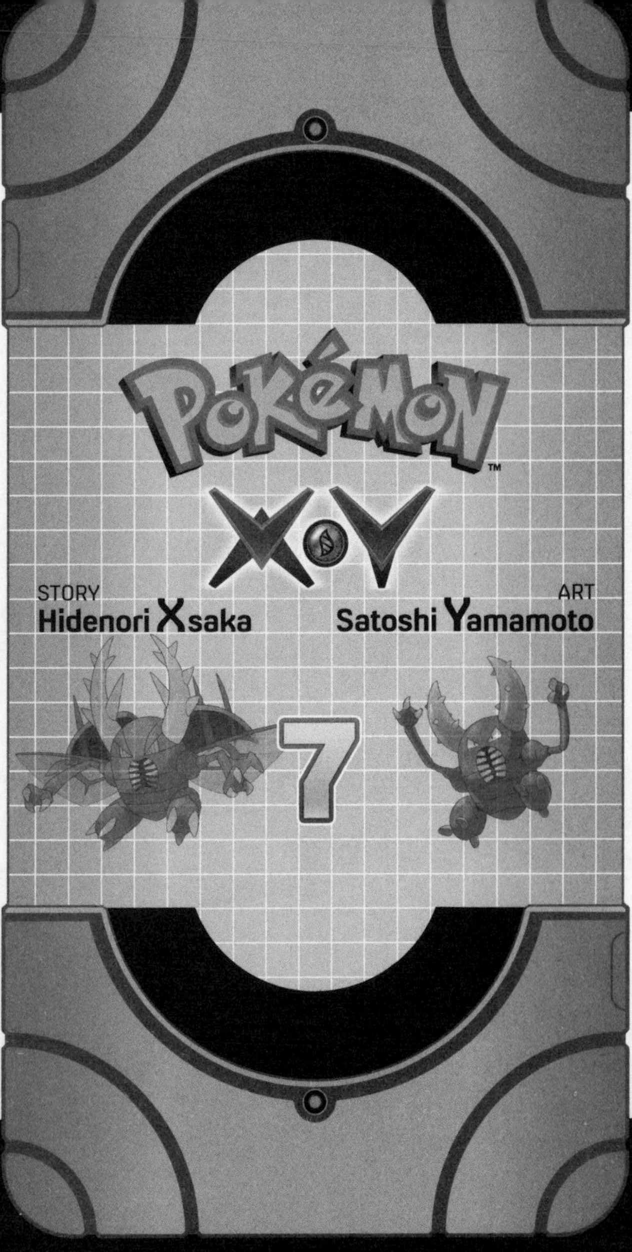

Pokémon™
X•Y
STORY
Hidenori Xsaka
ART
Satoshi Yamamoto
7

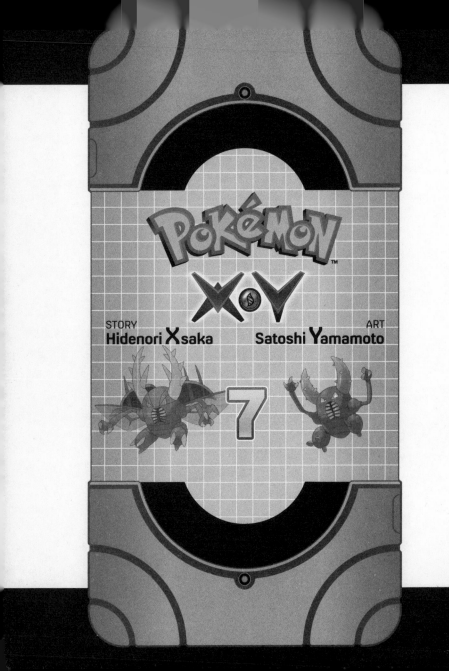

CHARACTERS

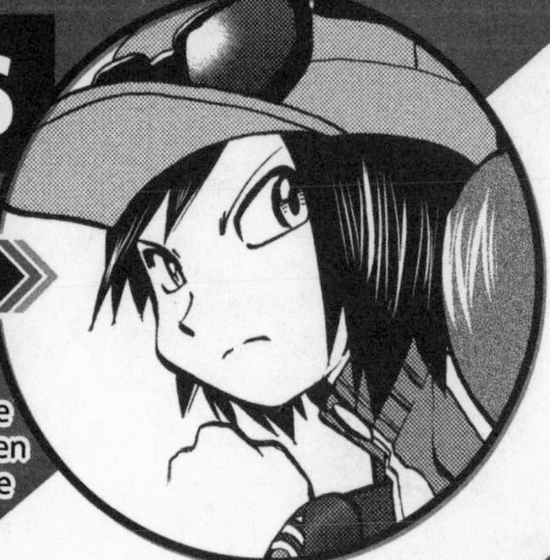

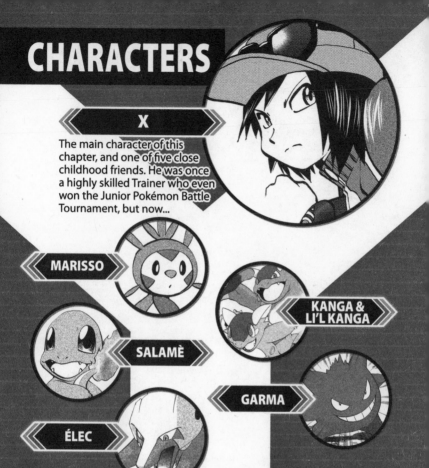

X

The main character of this chapter, and one of five close childhood friends. He was once a highly skilled Trainer who even won the Junior Pokémon Battle Tournament, but now...

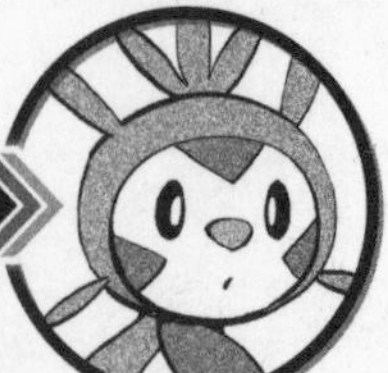

MARISSO

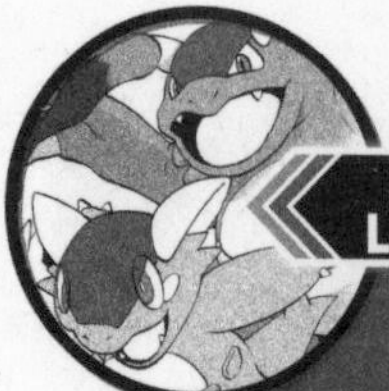

KANGA & LI'L KANGA

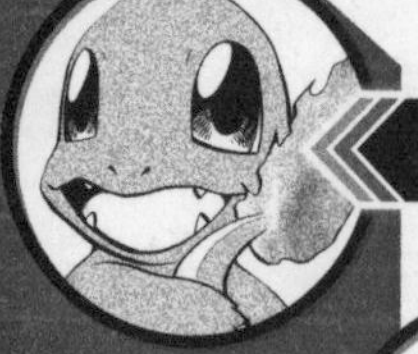

SALAMÈ

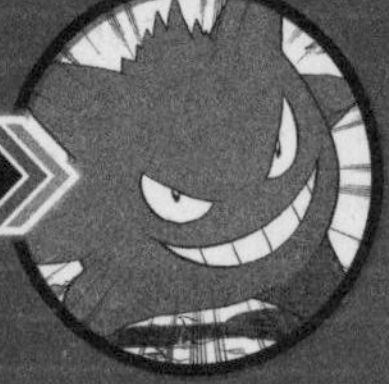

GARMA

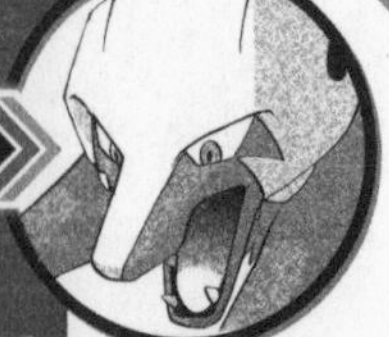

ÉLEC

OUR STORY THUS FAR...

In Vaniville Town in the Kalos region, X is a Pokémon Trainer child prodigy. But then he falls into a depression and hides in his room avoiding everyone. A sudden attack by the Legendary Pokémon Xerneas and Yveltal, controlled by Team Flare, forces X outside. Now he and his closest childhood friends—Y, Trevor, Tierno and Shauna—are on the run. X has a ring that Mega Evolves Pokémon and Team Flare wants to steal it. Turns out Team Flare has a nefarious plan to fire an ancient artifact called the Ultimate Weapon on the Kalos region and destroy it. Our friends launch an all-out attack to stop them, but Team Flare both escapes and steals Korrina's Key Stone!

MEET THE

Y

X's best friend, a Sky Trainer trainee. Her full name is Yvonne Gabena.

TREVOR

One of the five friends. A quiet boy who hopes to become a fine Pokémon Researcher one day.

SHAUNA

One of the five friends. Her dream is to become a Furfrou Groomer. She is quick to speak her mind.

TIERNO

One of the five friends. A big boy with an even bigger heart. He is currently training to become a dancer.

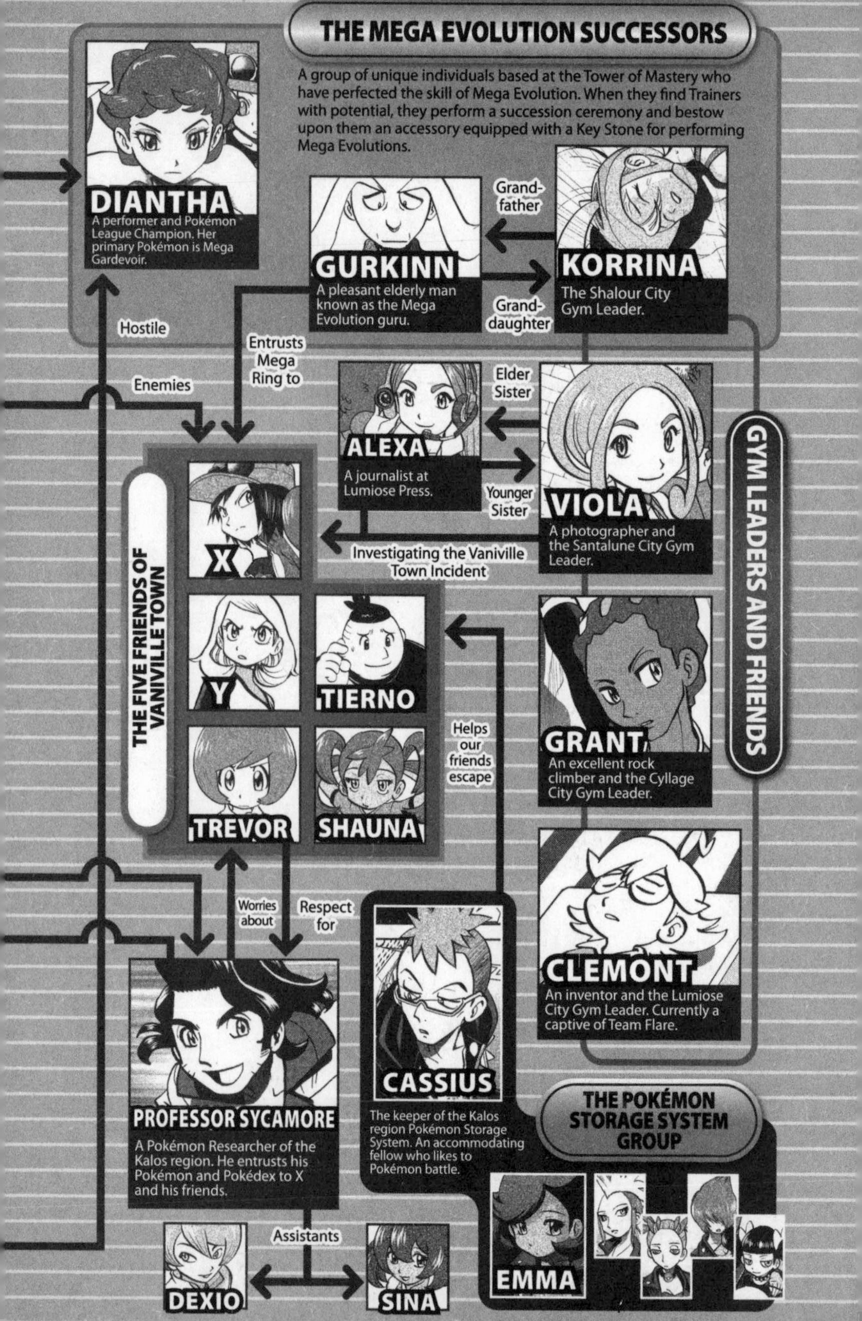
THE MEGA EVOLUTION SUCCESSORS
A group of unique individuals based at the Tower of Mastery who have perfected the skill of Mega Evolution. When they find Trainers with potential, they perform a succession ceremony and bestow upon them an accessory equipped with a Key Stone for performing Mega Evolutions.
DIANTHA
A performer and Pokémon League Champion. Her primary Pokémon is Mega Gardevoir.
GURKINN
A pleasant elderly man known as the Mega Evolution guru.
Grand-father
Grand-daughter
KORRINA
The Shalour City Gym Leader.
Hostile
Entrusts Mega Ring to
Enemies
GYM LEADERS AND FRIENDS
ALEXA
A journalist at Lumiose Press.
Elder Sister
Younger Sister
VIOLA
A photographer and the Santalune City Gym Leader.
Investigating the Vaniville Town Incident
THE FIVE FRIENDS OF VANIVILLE TOWN
X
Y
TIERNO
TREVOR
SHAUNA
Helps our friends escape
GRANT
An excellent rock climber and the Cyllage City Gym Leader.
CLEMONT
An inventor and the Lumiose City Gym Leader. Currently a captive of Team Flare.
Worries about
Respect for
PROFESSOR SYCAMORE
A Pokémon Researcher of the Kalos region. He entrusts his Pokémon and Pokédex to X and his friends.
CASSIUS
The keeper of the Kalos region Pokémon Storage System. An accommodating fellow who likes to Pokémon battle.
THE POKÉMON STORAGE SYSTEM GROUP
EMMA
Assistants
DEXIO
SINA

CHARACTER CORRELATION CHART

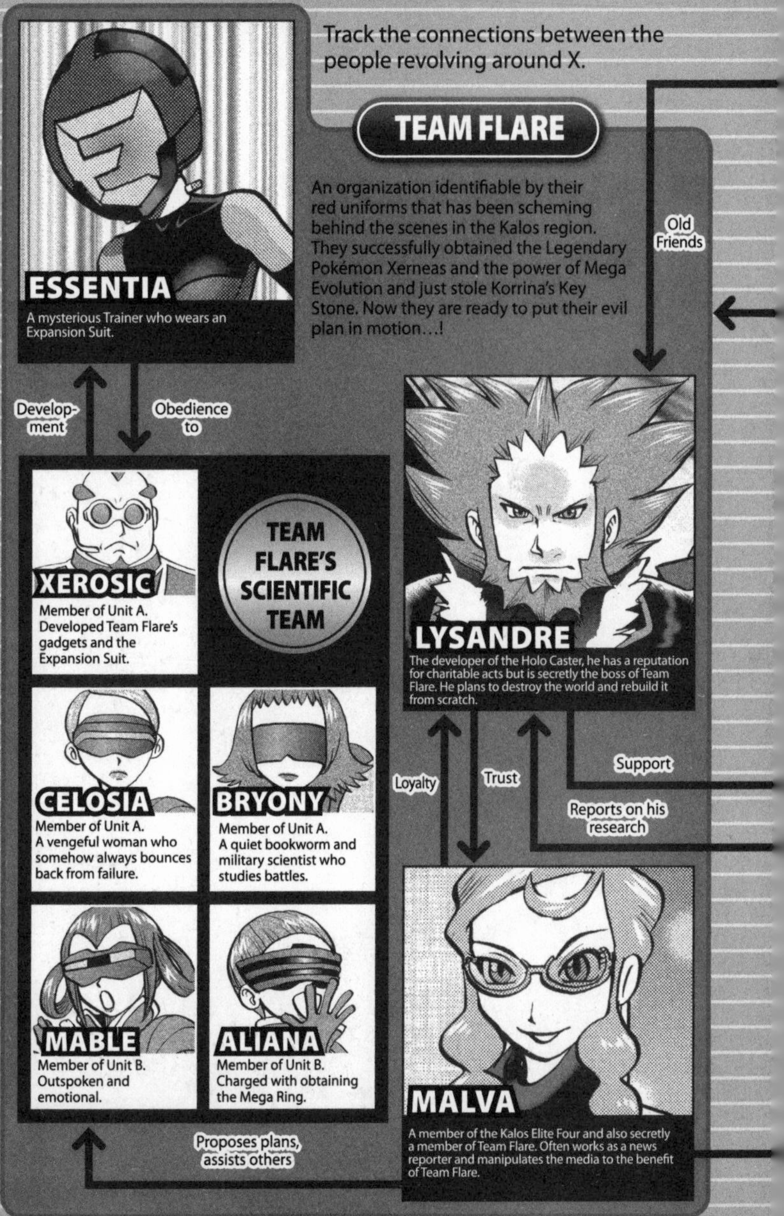
Track the connections between the people revolving around X.
TEAM FLARE
An organization identifiable by their red uniforms that has been scheming behind the scenes in the Kalos region. They successfully obtained the Legendary Pokémon Xerneas and the power of Mega Evolution and just stole Korrina's Key Stone. Now they are ready to put their evil plan in motion…!
ESSENTIA
A mysterious Trainer who wears an Expansion Suit.
Old Friends
Develop-ment
Obedience to
TEAM FLARE'S SCIENTIFIC TEAM
XEROSIC
Member of Unit A. Developed Team Flare's gadgets and the Expansion Suit.
LYSANDRE
The developer of the Holo Caster, he has a reputation for charitable acts but is secretly the boss of Team Flare. He plans to destroy the world and rebuild it from scratch.
CELOSIA
Member of Unit A. A vengeful woman who somehow always bounces back from failure.
BRYONY
Member of Unit A. A quiet bookworm and military scientist who studies battles.
Loyalty
Trust
Support
Reports on his research
MABLE
Member of Unit B. Outspoken and emotional.
ALIANA
Member of Unit B. Charged with obtaining the Mega Ring.
MALVA
A member of the Kalos Elite Four and also secretly a member of Team Flare. Often works as a news reporter and manipulates the media to the benefit of Team Flare.
Proposes plans, assists others

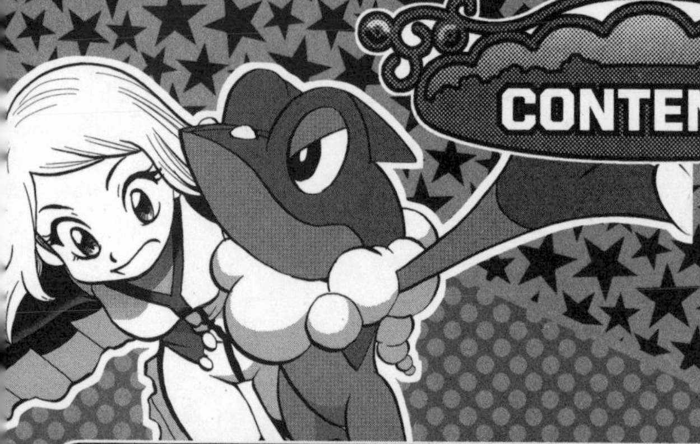

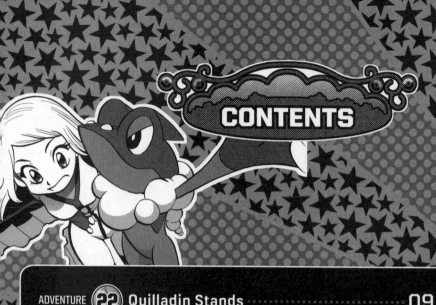

CONTENTS

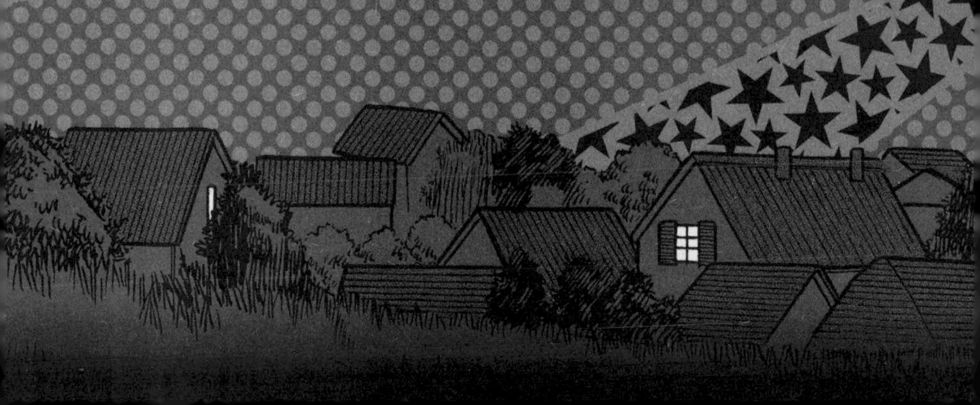

Adventure 22 Quilladin Stands

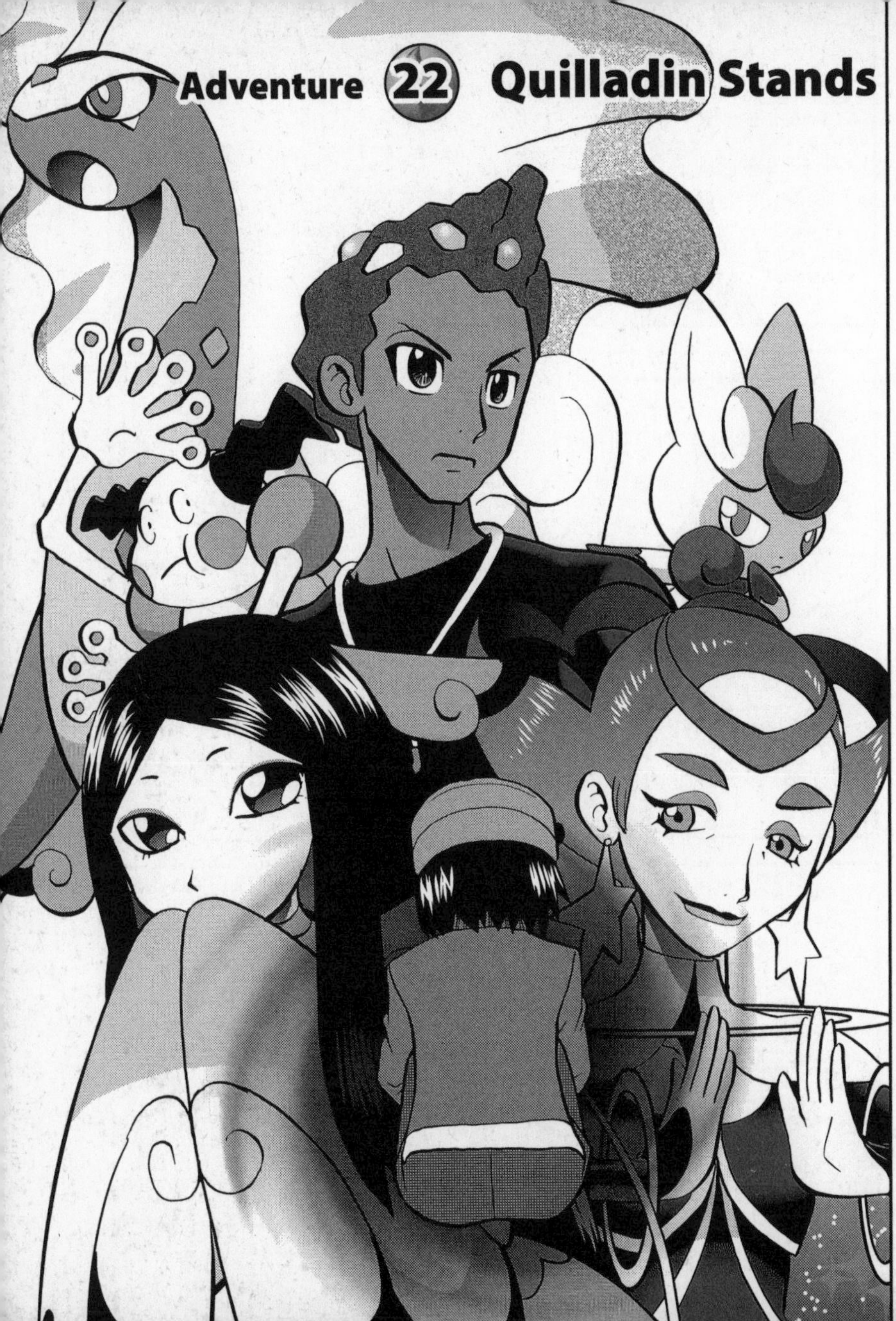

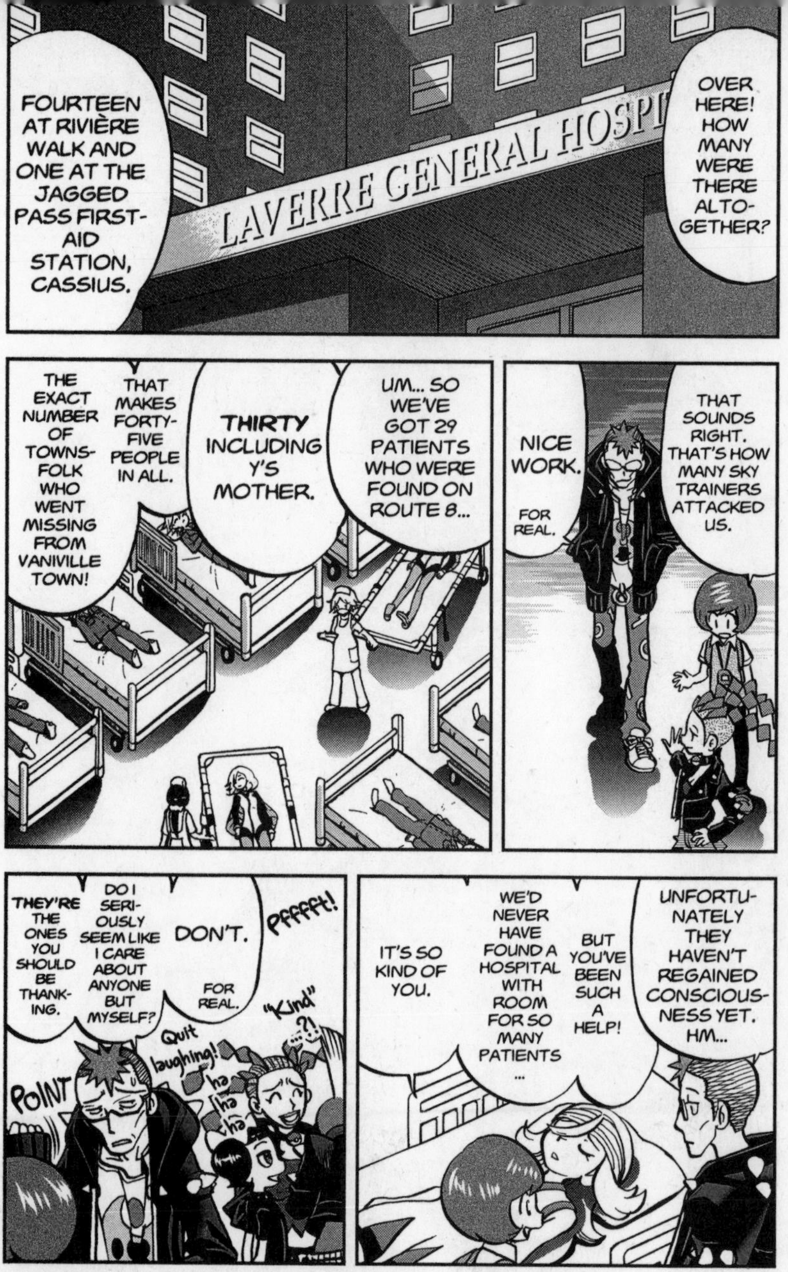
OVER HERE! HOW MANY WERE THERE ALTOGETHER?
FOURTEEN AT RIVIÈRE WALK AND ONE AT THE JAGGED PASS FIRST-AID STATION, CASSIUS.
THAT SOUNDS RIGHT. THAT'S HOW MANY SKY TRAINERS ATTACKED US.
NICE WORK.
FOR REAL.
UM... SO WE'VE GOT 29 PATIENTS WHO WERE FOUND ON ROUTE 8...
THIRTY INCLUDING Y'S MOTHER.
THAT MAKES FORTY-FIVE PEOPLE IN ALL.
THE EXACT NUMBER OF TOWNSFOLK WHO WENT MISSING FROM VANIVILLE TOWN!
UNFORTUNATELY THEY HAVEN'T REGAINED CONSCIOUSNESS YET. HM...
BUT YOU'VE BEEN SUCH A HELP!
WE'D NEVER HAVE FOUND A HOSPITAL WITH ROOM FOR SO MANY PATIENTS...
IT'S SO KIND OF YOU.
Pfffft!
DON'T.
FOR REAL.
DO I SERIOUSLY SEEM LIKE I CARE ABOUT ANYONE BUT MYSELF?
THEY'RE THE ONES YOU SHOULD BE THANKING.
"Kind"...?!
Quit laughing!
ha ha ha
POINT

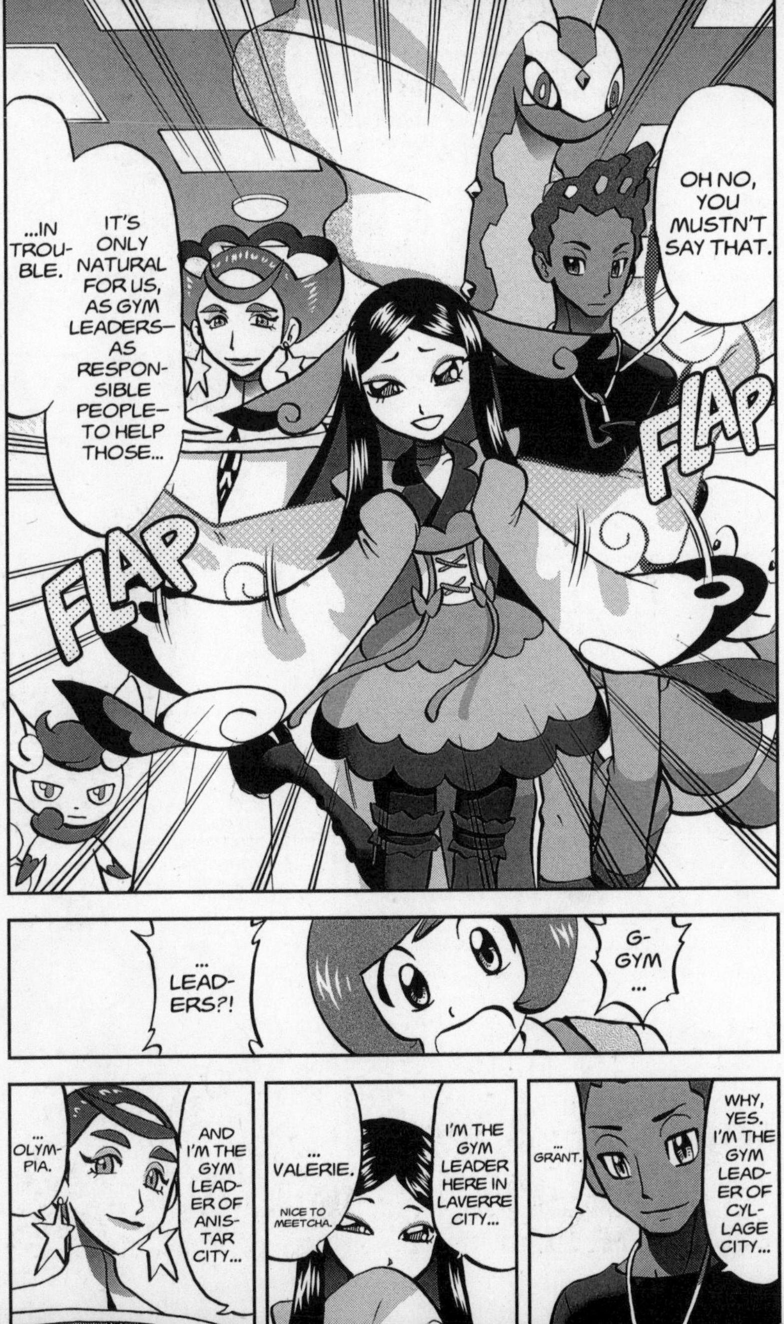
OH NO, YOU MUSTN'T SAY THAT.
FLAP
IT'S ONLY NATURAL FOR US, AS GYM LEADERS—AS RESPONSIBLE PEOPLE—TO HELP THOSE...
...IN TROUBLE.
FLAP
G-GYM...
...LEADERS?!
WHY, YES. I'M THE GYM LEADER OF CYLLAGE CITY...
...GRANT.
I'M THE GYM LEADER HERE IN LAVERRE CITY...
...VALERIE.
NICE TO MEETCHA.
AND I'M THE GYM LEADER OF ANISTAR CITY...
...OLYMPIA.

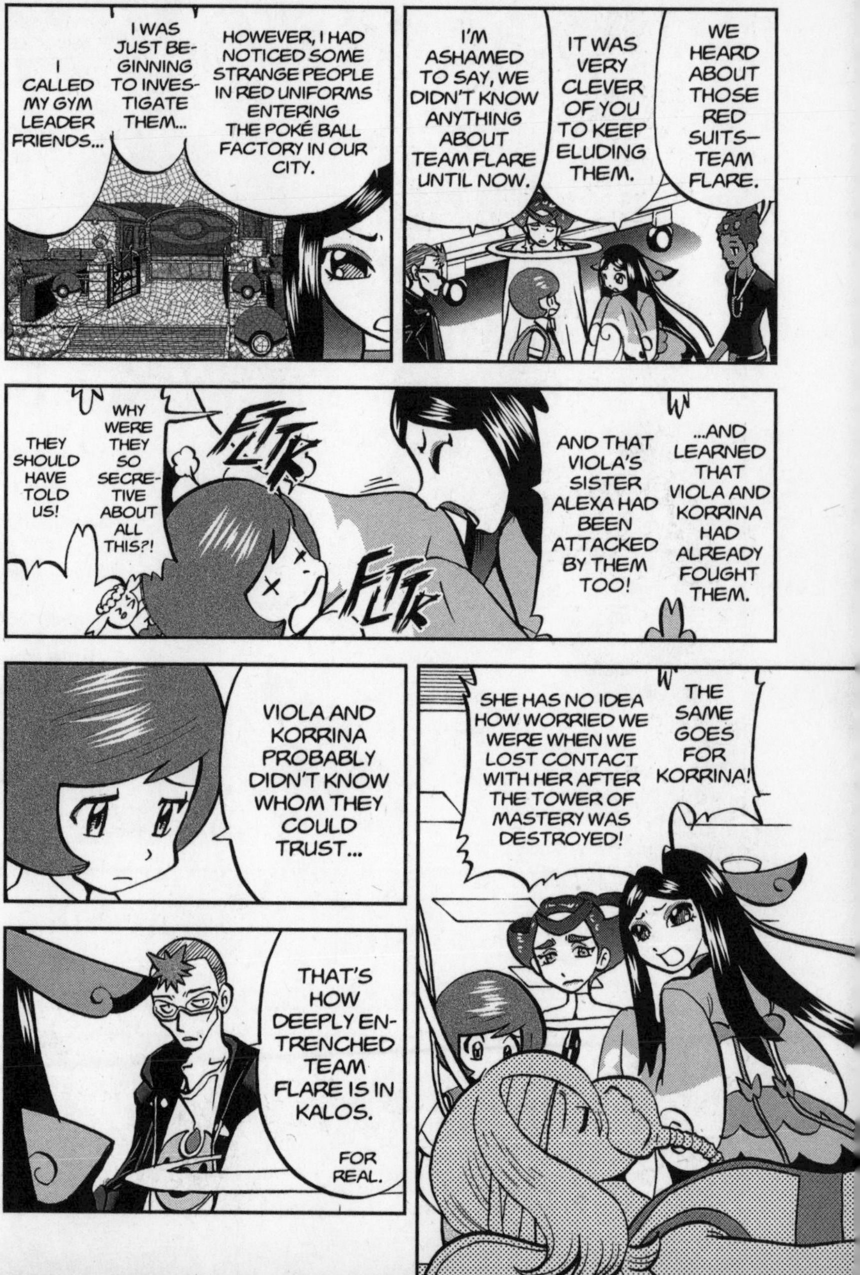
WE HEARD ABOUT THOSE RED SUITS—TEAM FLARE.
IT WAS VERY CLEVER OF YOU TO KEEP ELUDING THEM.
I'M ASHAMED TO SAY, WE DIDN'T KNOW ANYTHING ABOUT TEAM FLARE UNTIL NOW.
HOWEVER, I HAD NOTICED SOME STRANGE PEOPLE IN RED UNIFORMS ENTERING THE POKÉ BALL FACTORY IN OUR CITY.
I WAS JUST BEGINNING TO INVESTIGATE THEM...
I CALLED MY GYM LEADER FRIENDS...
...AND LEARNED THAT VIOLA AND KORRINA HAD ALREADY FOUGHT THEM.
AND THAT VIOLA'S SISTER ALEXA HAD BEEN ATTACKED BY THEM TOO!
FLTR
FLTR
WHY WERE THEY SO SECRETIVE ABOUT ALL THIS?!
THEY SHOULD HAVE TOLD US!
THE SAME GOES FOR KORRINA!
SHE HAS NO IDEA HOW WORRIED WE WERE WHEN WE LOST CONTACT WITH HER AFTER THE TOWER OF MASTERY WAS DESTROYED!
VIOLA AND KORRINA PROBABLY DIDN'T KNOW WHOM THEY COULD TRUST...
THAT'S HOW DEEPLY ENTRENCHED TEAM FLARE IS IN KALOS.
FOR REAL.

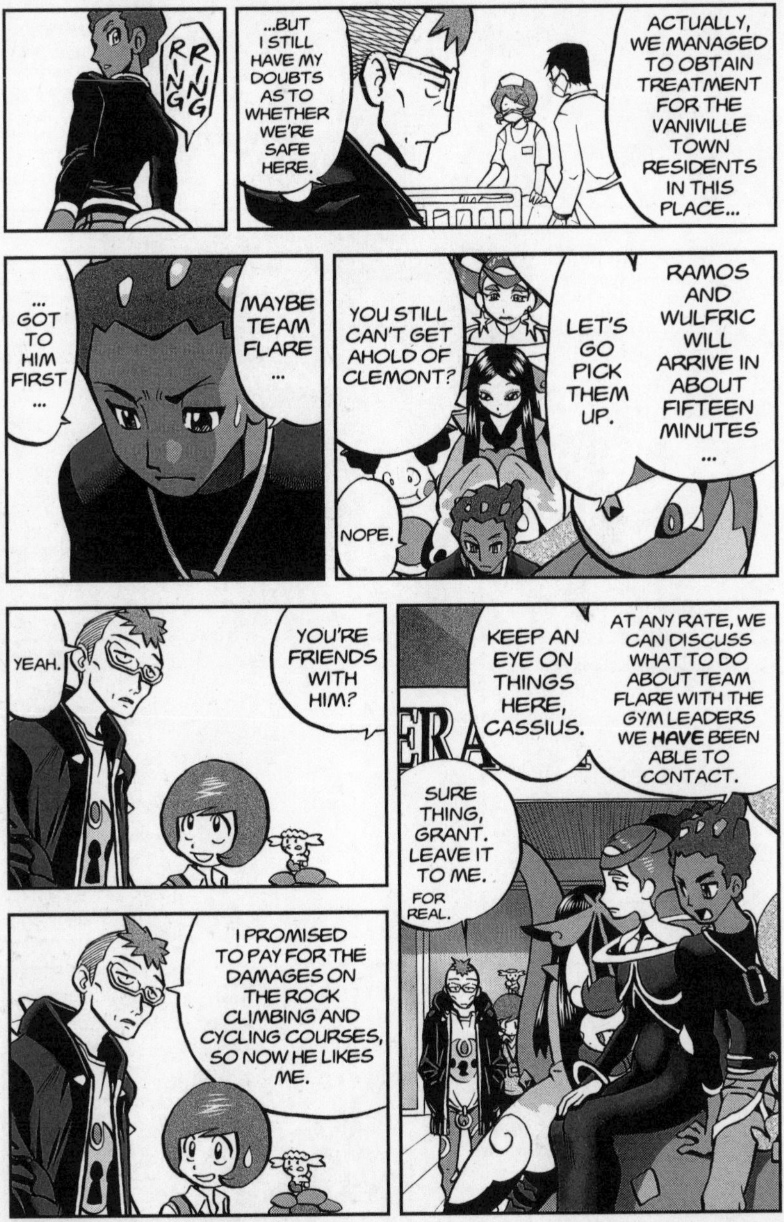
ACTUALLY, WE MANAGED TO OBTAIN TREATMENT FOR THE VANIVILLE TOWN RESIDENTS IN THIS PLACE...
...BUT I STILL HAVE MY DOUBTS AS TO WHETHER WE'RE SAFE HERE.
RRING RRING
RAMOS AND WULFRIC WILL ARRIVE IN ABOUT FIFTEEN MINUTES...
LET'S GO PICK THEM UP.
YOU STILL CAN'T GET AHOLD OF CLEMONT?
NOPE.
MAYBE TEAM FLARE...
...GOT TO HIM FIRST...
AT ANY RATE, WE CAN DISCUSS WHAT TO DO ABOUT TEAM FLARE WITH THE GYM LEADERS WE **HAVE** BEEN ABLE TO CONTACT.
KEEP AN EYE ON THINGS HERE, CASSIUS.
SURE THING, GRANT. LEAVE IT TO ME.
FOR REAL.
YOU'RE FRIENDS WITH HIM?
YEAH.
I PROMISED TO PAY FOR THE DAMAGES ON THE ROCK CLIMBING AND CYCLING COURSES, SO NOW HE LIKES ME.

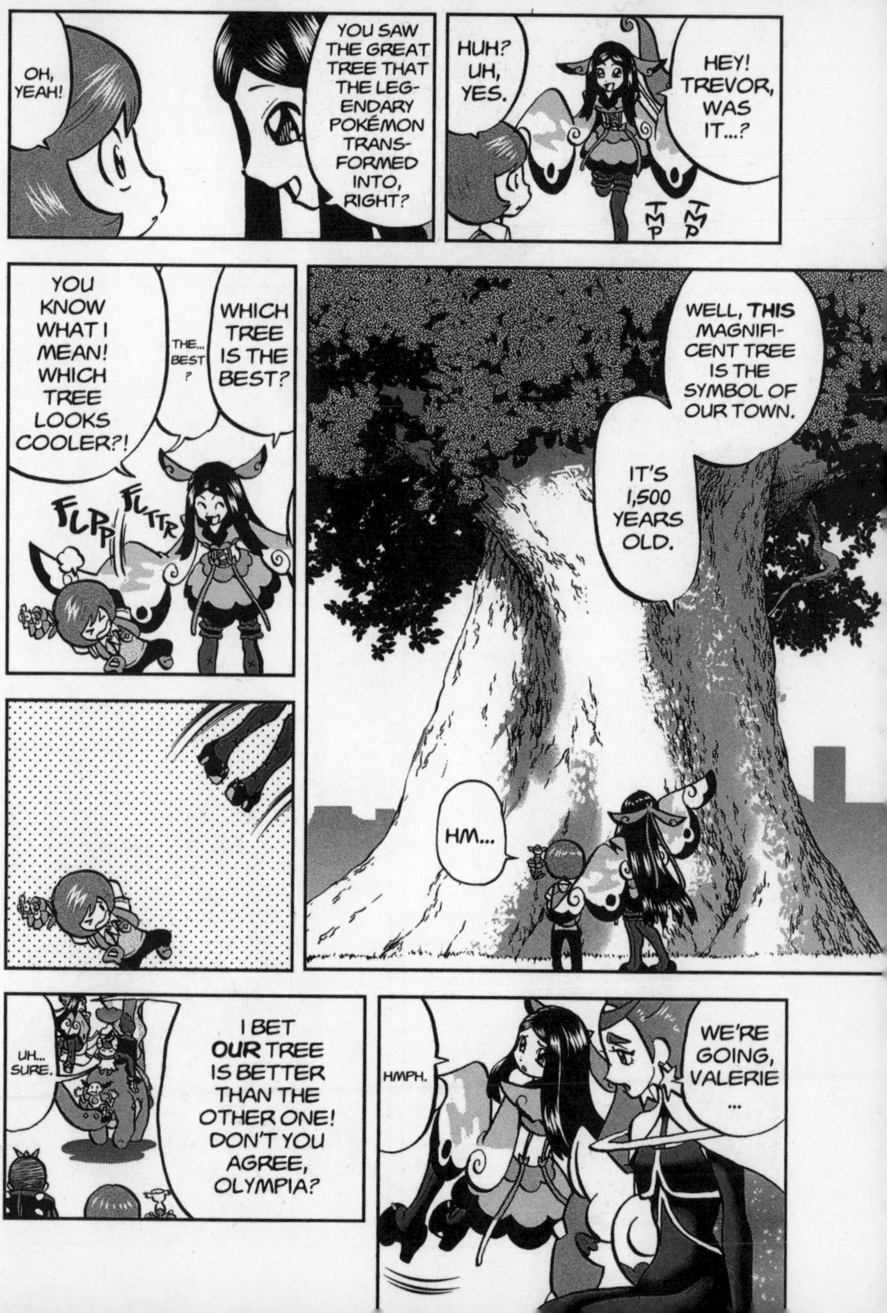
HEY! TREVOR, WAS IT...?
HUH? UH, YES.
TMP TMP
YOU SAW THE GREAT TREE THAT THE LEGENDARY POKÉMON TRANSFORMED INTO, RIGHT?
OH, YEAH!
WELL, **THIS** MAGNIFICENT TREE IS THE SYMBOL OF OUR TOWN.
IT'S 1,500 YEARS OLD.
HM...
WHICH TREE IS THE BEST?
THE... BEST?
YOU KNOW WHAT I MEAN! WHICH TREE LOOKS COOLER?!
FLUTTR
FLPP
WE'RE GOING, VALERIE...
HMPH.
I BET **OUR** TREE IS BETTER THAN THE OTHER ONE! DON'T YOU AGREE, OLYMPIA?
UH... SURE.

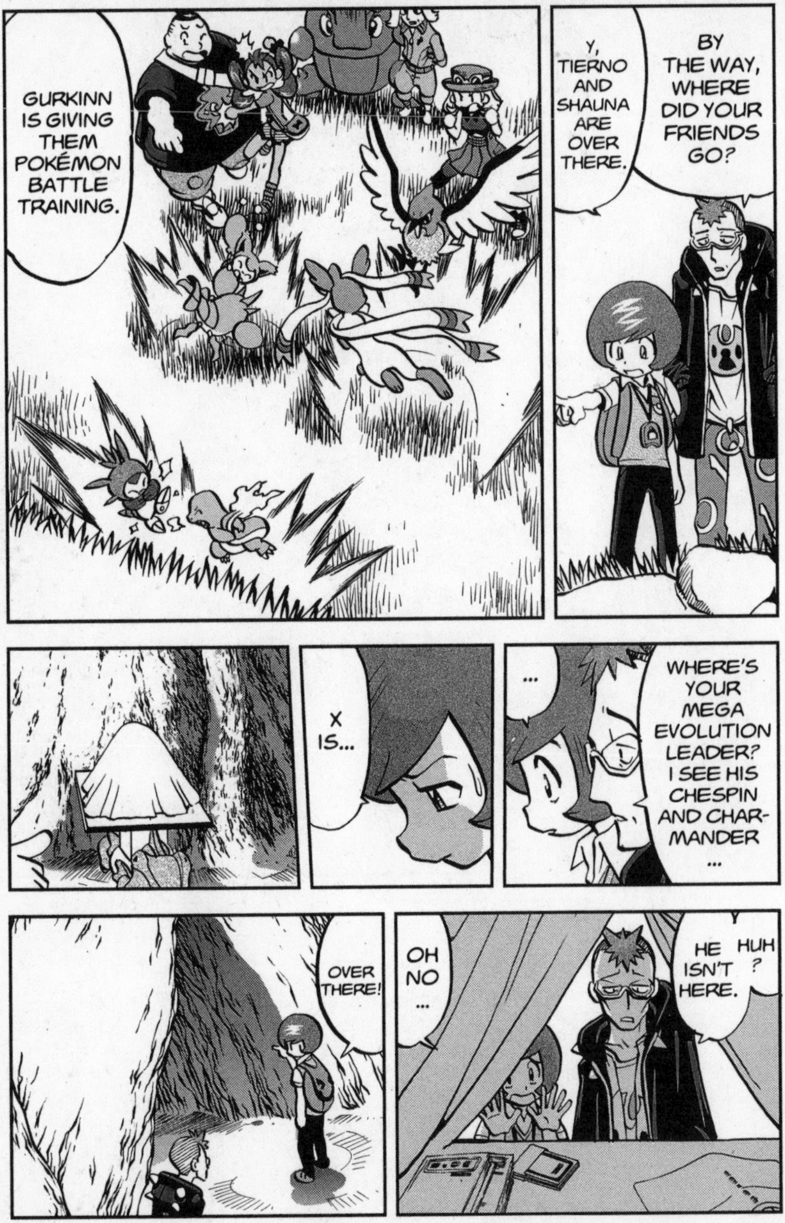
BY THE WAY, WHERE DID YOUR FRIENDS GO?
Y, TIERNO AND SHAUNA ARE OVER THERE.
GURKINN IS GIVING THEM POKÉMON BATTLE TRAINING.
WHERE'S YOUR MEGA EVOLUTION LEADER? I SEE HIS CHESPIN AND CHARMANDER ...
...
X IS...
HUH ?
HE ISN'T HERE.
OH NO ...
OVER THERE!

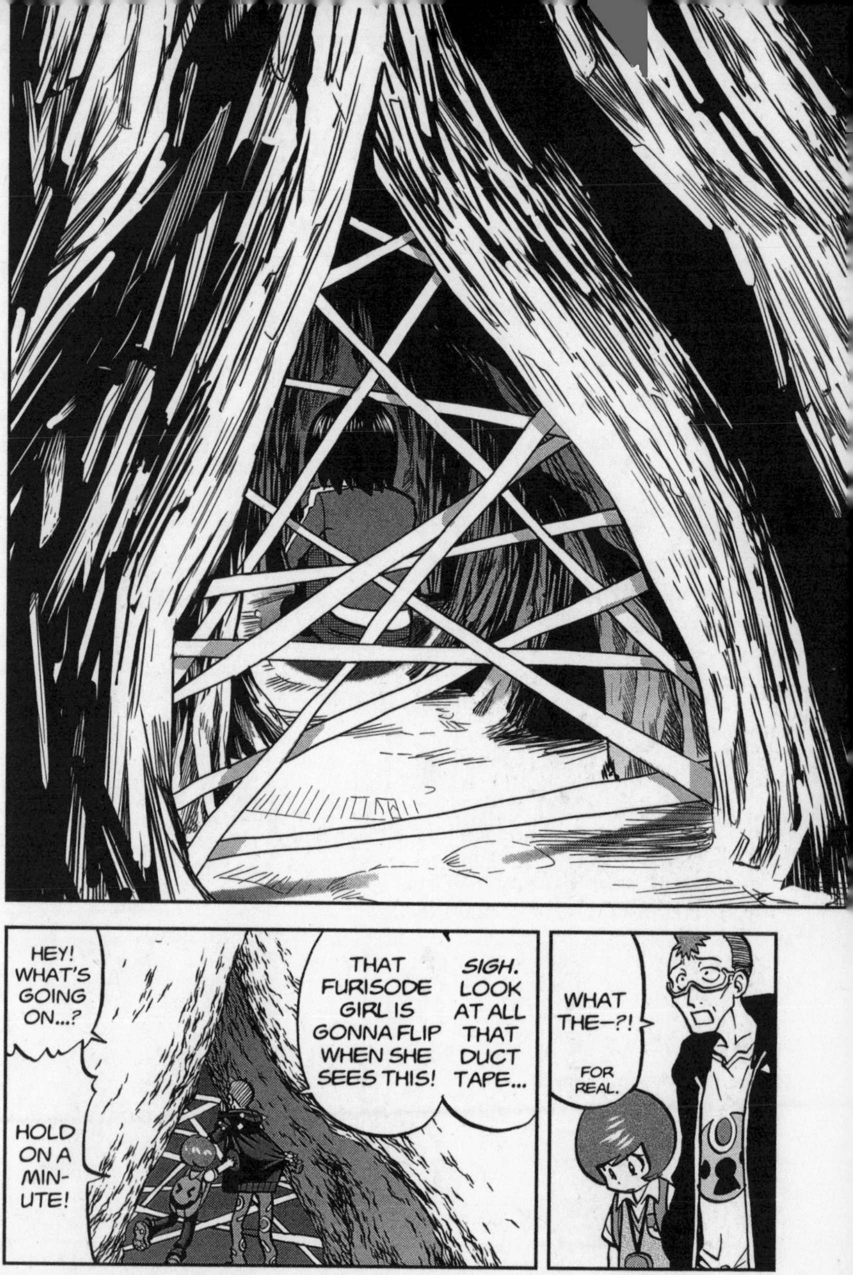
WHAT THE–?!
FOR REAL.
SIGH. LOOK AT ALL THAT DUCT TAPE...
THAT FURISODE GIRL IS GONNA FLIP WHEN SHE SEES THIS!
HEY! WHAT'S GOING ON...?
HOLD ON A MIN-UTE!

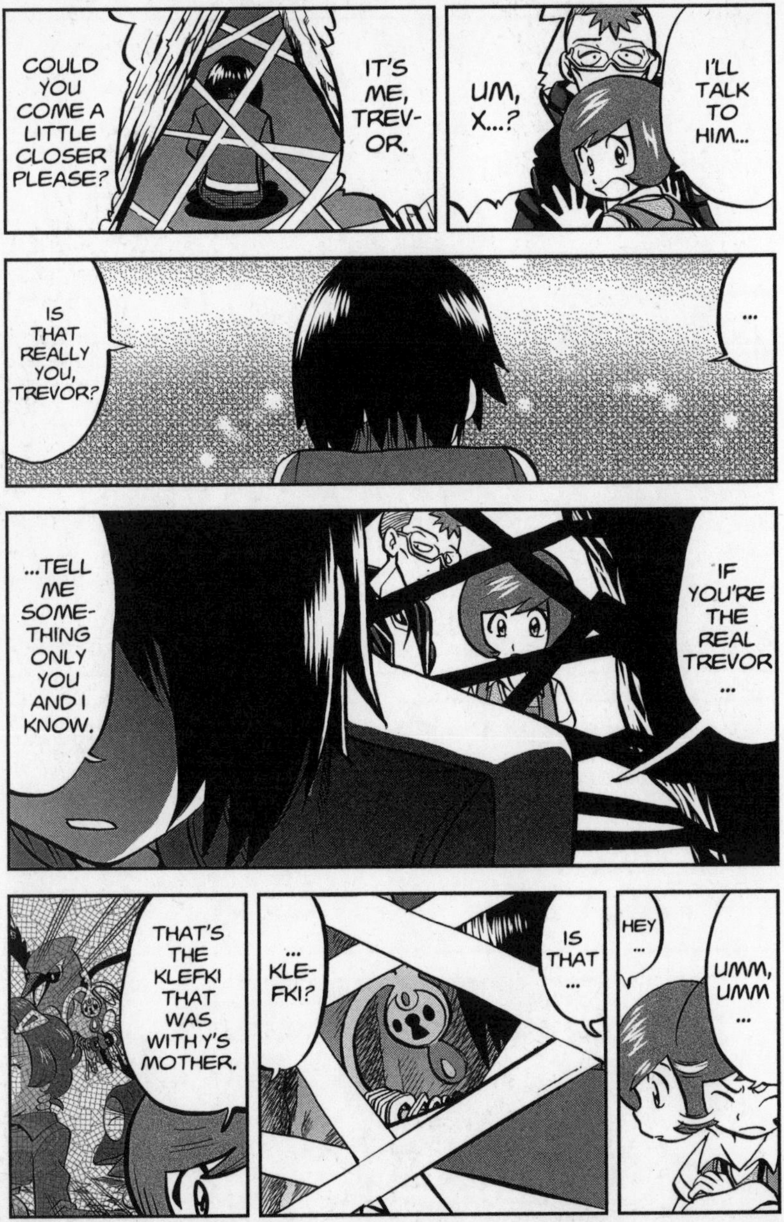
I'LL TALK TO HIM...
UM, X...?
IT'S ME, TREV-OR.
COULD YOU COME A LITTLE CLOSER PLEASE?
...
IS THAT REALLY YOU, TREVOR?
IF YOU'RE THE REAL TREVOR...
...TELL ME SOME-THING ONLY YOU AND I KNOW.
UMM, UMM...
HEY...
IS THAT...
...KLE-FKI?
THAT'S THE KLEFKI THAT WAS WITH Y'S MOTHER.

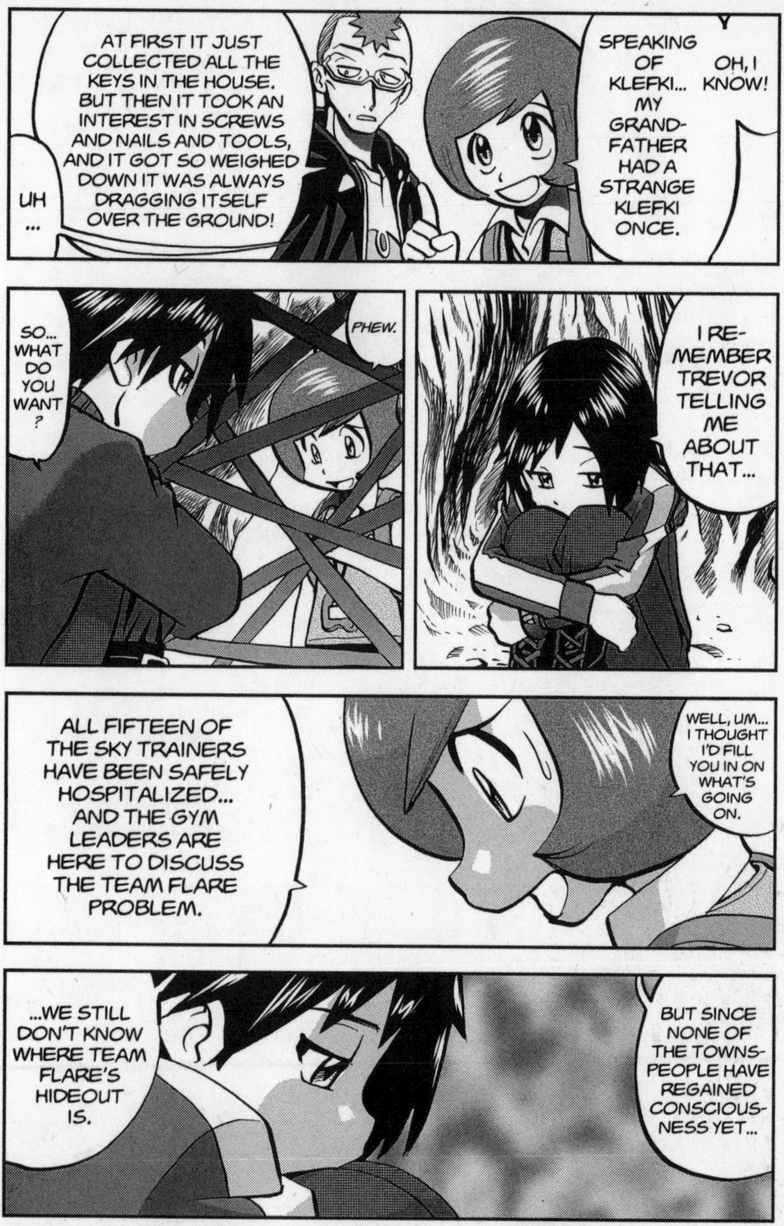
OH, I KNOW!
SPEAKING OF KLEFKI... MY GRANDFATHER HAD A STRANGE KLEFKI ONCE.
AT FIRST IT JUST COLLECTED ALL THE KEYS IN THE HOUSE. BUT THEN IT TOOK AN INTEREST IN SCREWS AND NAILS AND TOOLS, AND IT GOT SO WEIGHED DOWN IT WAS ALWAYS DRAGGING ITSELF OVER THE GROUND!
UH ...
I RE-MEMBER TREVOR TELLING ME ABOUT THAT...
PHEW.
SO... WHAT DO YOU WANT?
WELL, UM... I THOUGHT I'D FILL YOU IN ON WHAT'S GOING ON.
ALL FIFTEEN OF THE SKY TRAINERS HAVE BEEN SAFELY HOSPITALIZED... AND THE GYM LEADERS ARE HERE TO DISCUSS THE TEAM FLARE PROBLEM.
BUT SINCE NONE OF THE TOWNS-PEOPLE HAVE REGAINED CONSCIOUS-NESS YET...
...WE STILL DON'T KNOW WHERE TEAM FLARE'S HIDEOUT IS.

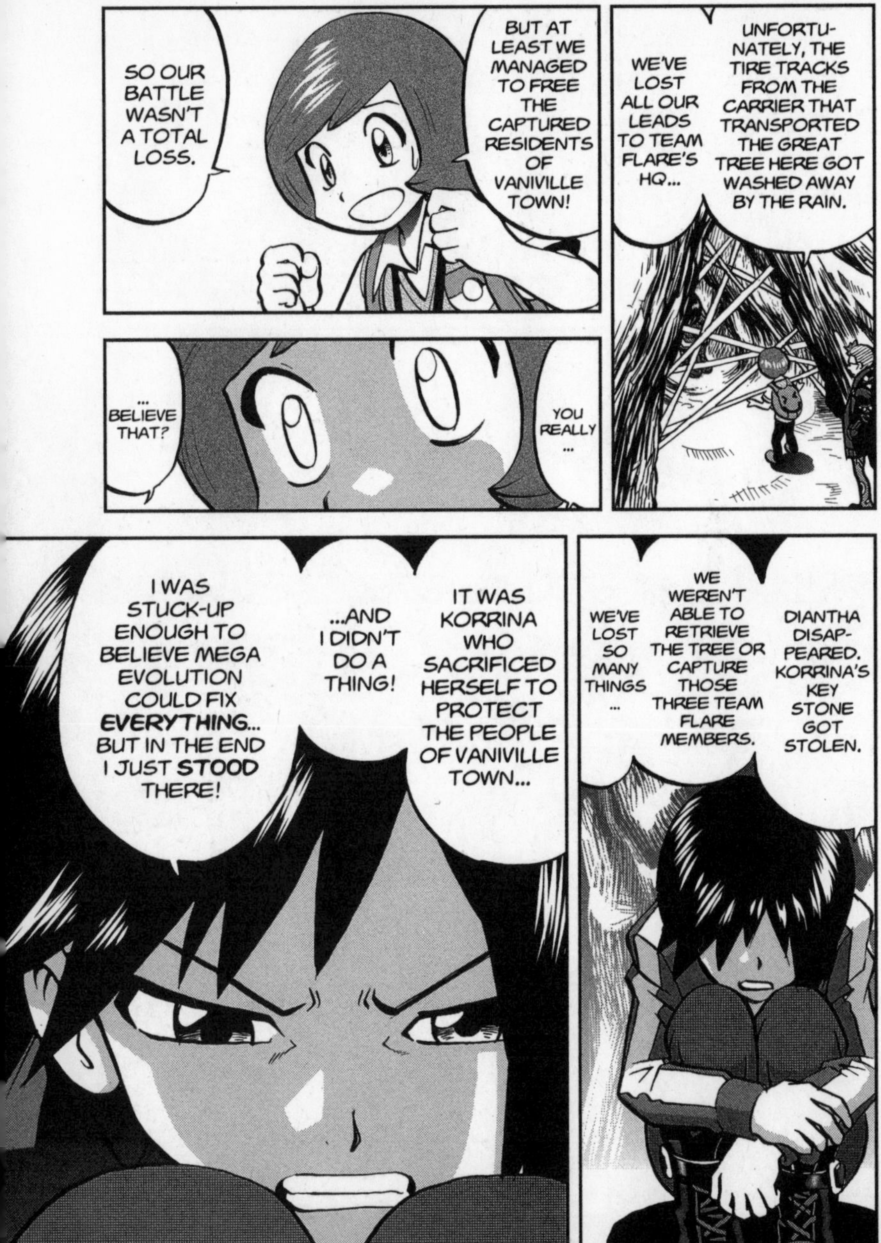
UNFORTUNATELY, THE TIRE TRACKS FROM THE CARRIER THAT TRANSPORTED THE GREAT TREE HERE GOT WASHED AWAY BY THE RAIN.
WE'VE LOST ALL OUR LEADS TO TEAM FLARE'S HQ...
BUT AT LEAST WE MANAGED TO FREE THE CAPTURED RESIDENTS OF VANIVILLE TOWN!
SO OUR BATTLE WASN'T A TOTAL LOSS.
YOU REALLY...
...BELIEVE THAT?
DIANTHA DISAPPEARED. KORRINA'S KEY STONE GOT STOLEN.
WE WEREN'T ABLE TO RETRIEVE THE TREE OR CAPTURE THOSE THREE TEAM FLARE MEMBERS.
WE'VE LOST SO MANY THINGS...
IT WAS KORRINA WHO SACRIFICED HERSELF TO PROTECT THE PEOPLE OF VANIVILLE TOWN...
...AND I DIDN'T DO A THING!
I WAS STUCK-UP ENOUGH TO BELIEVE MEGA EVOLUTION COULD FIX EVERYTHING... BUT IN THE END I JUST STOOD THERE!

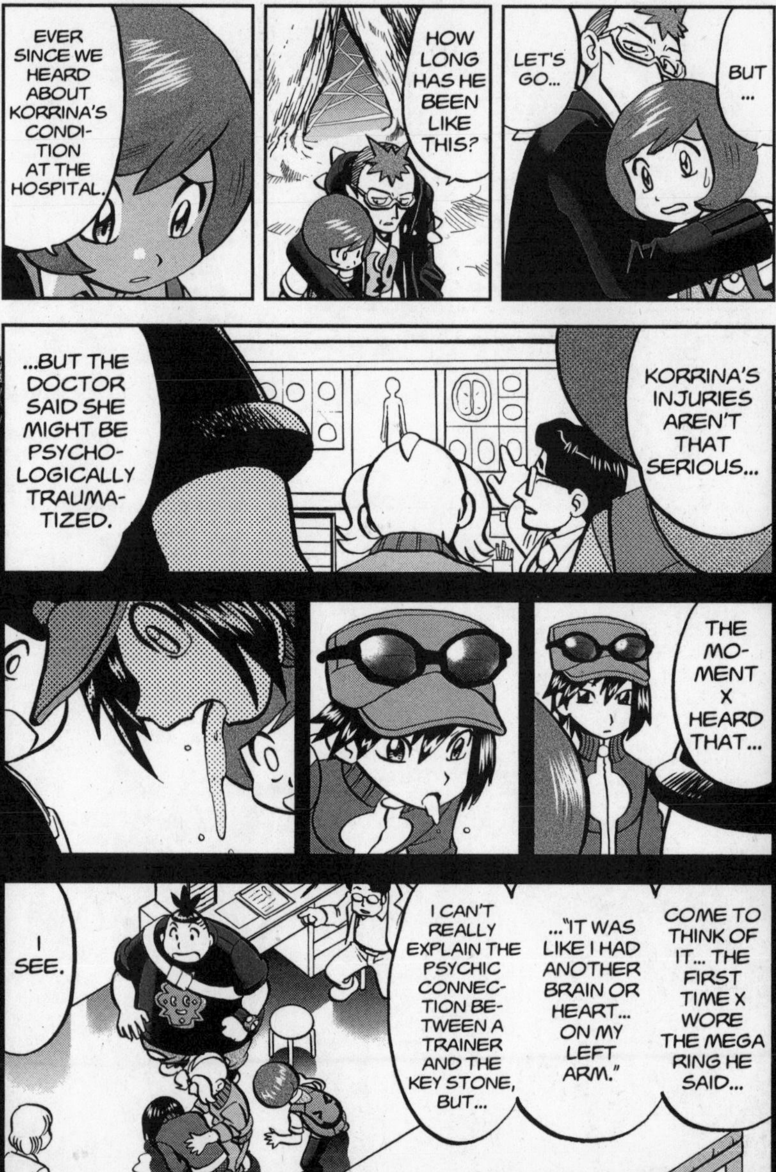
LET'S GO...
BUT ...
HOW LONG HAS HE BEEN LIKE THIS?
EVER SINCE WE HEARD ABOUT KORRINA'S CONDITION AT THE HOSPITAL.
KORRINA'S INJURIES AREN'T THAT SERIOUS...
...BUT THE DOCTOR SAID SHE MIGHT BE PSYCHOLOGICALLY TRAUMATIZED.
THE MOMENT X HEARD THAT...
COME TO THINK OF IT... THE FIRST TIME X WORE THE MEGA RING HE SAID...
..."IT WAS LIKE I HAD ANOTHER BRAIN OR HEART... ON MY LEFT ARM."
I CAN'T REALLY EXPLAIN THE PSYCHIC CONNECTION BETWEEN A TRAINER AND THE KEY STONE, BUT...
I SEE.

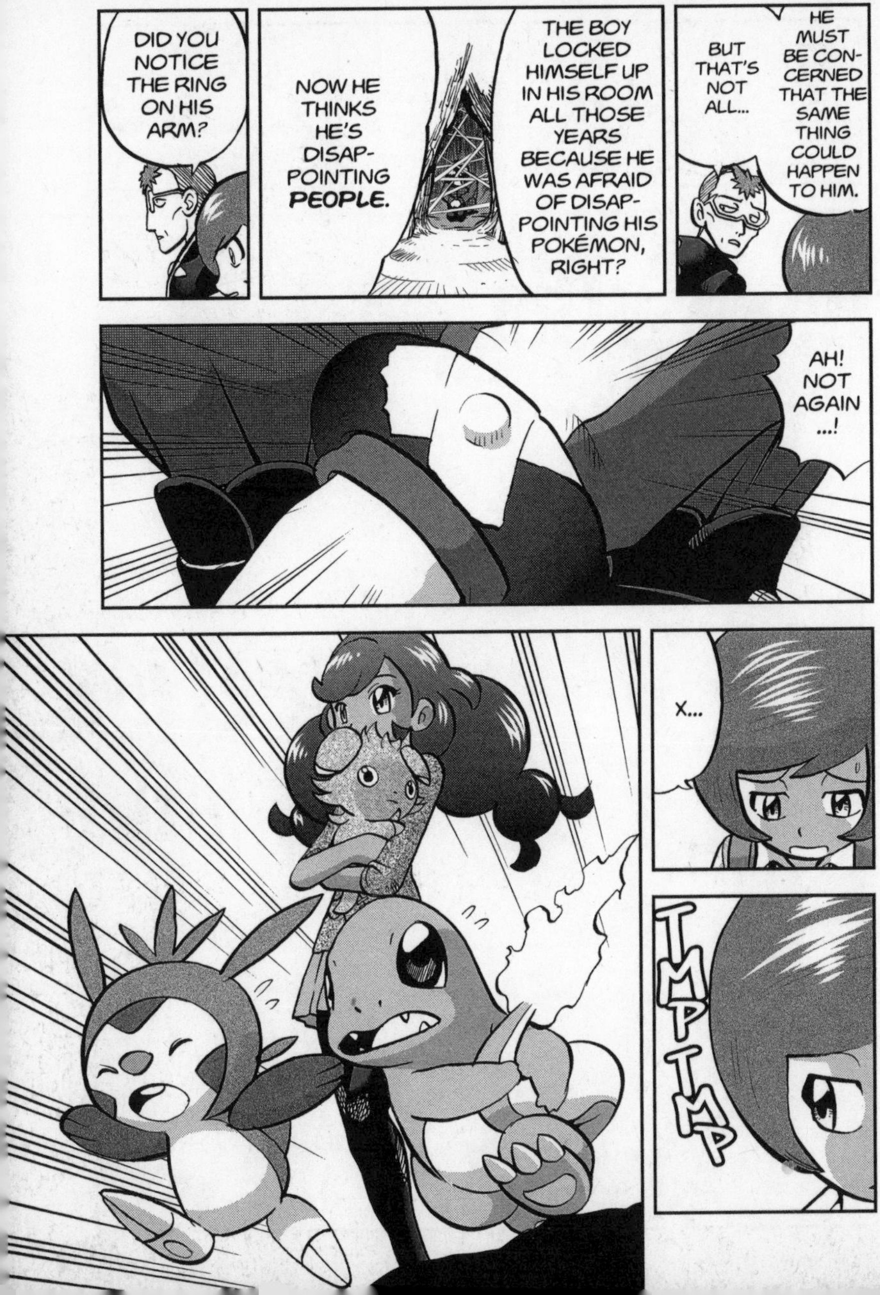
HE MUST BE CON-CERNED THAT THE SAME THING COULD HAPPEN TO HIM.
BUT THAT'S NOT ALL...
THE BOY LOCKED HIMSELF UP IN HIS ROOM ALL THOSE YEARS BECAUSE HE WAS AFRAID OF DISAP-POINTING HIS POKÉMON, RIGHT?
NOW HE THINKS HE'S DISAP-POINTING **PEOPLE**.
DID YOU NOTICE THE RING ON HIS ARM?
AH! NOT AGAIN ...!
X...
TMP TMP

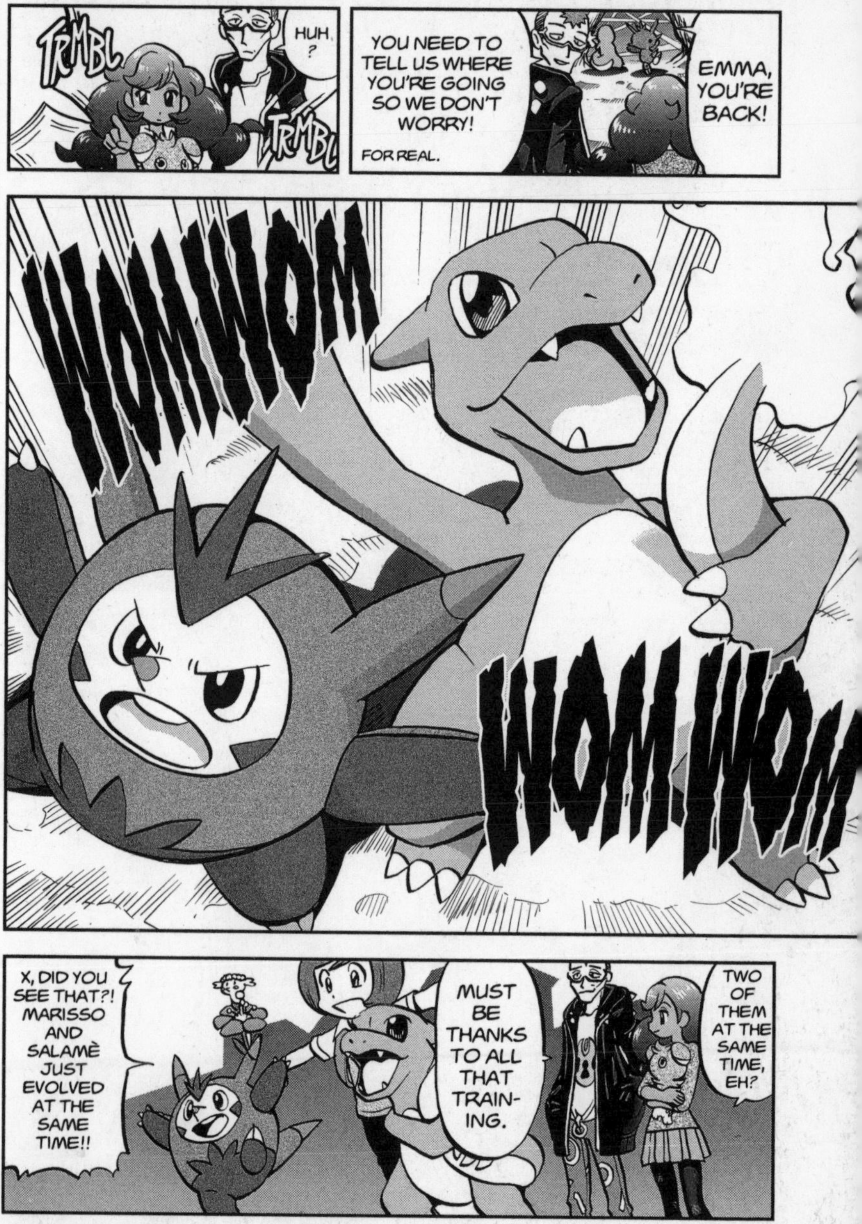
EMMA, YOU'RE BACK!
YOU NEED TO TELL US WHERE YOU'RE GOING SO WE DON'T WORRY!
FOR REAL.
HUH ?
TRMBL
TRMBL
WOM WOM
WOM WOM
TWO OF THEM AT THE SAME TIME, EH?
MUST BE THANKS TO ALL THAT TRAIN-ING.
X, DID YOU SEE THAT?! MARISSO AND SALAMÈ JUST EVOLVED AT THE SAME TIME!!

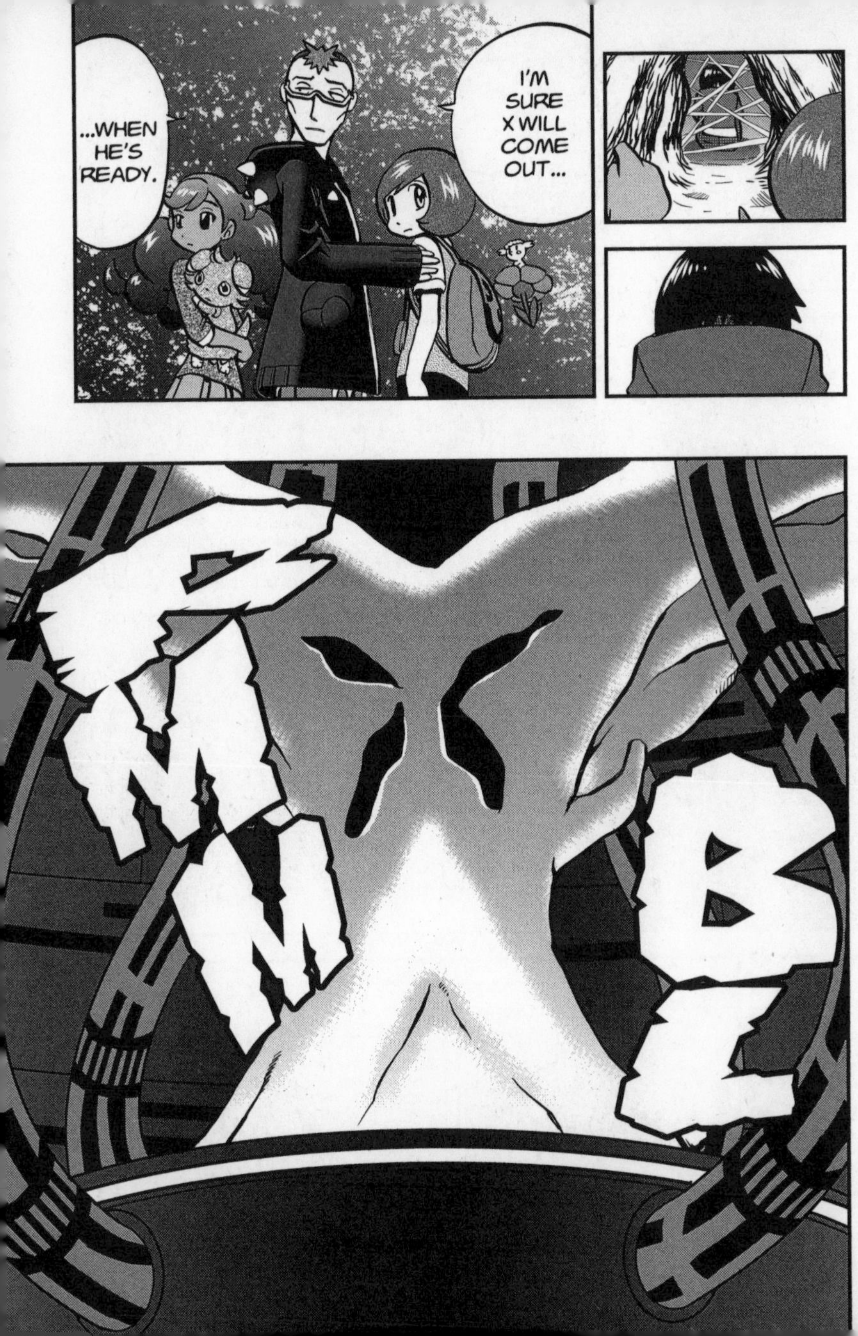
I'M SURE X WILL COME OUT...
...WHEN HE'S READY.
MMB

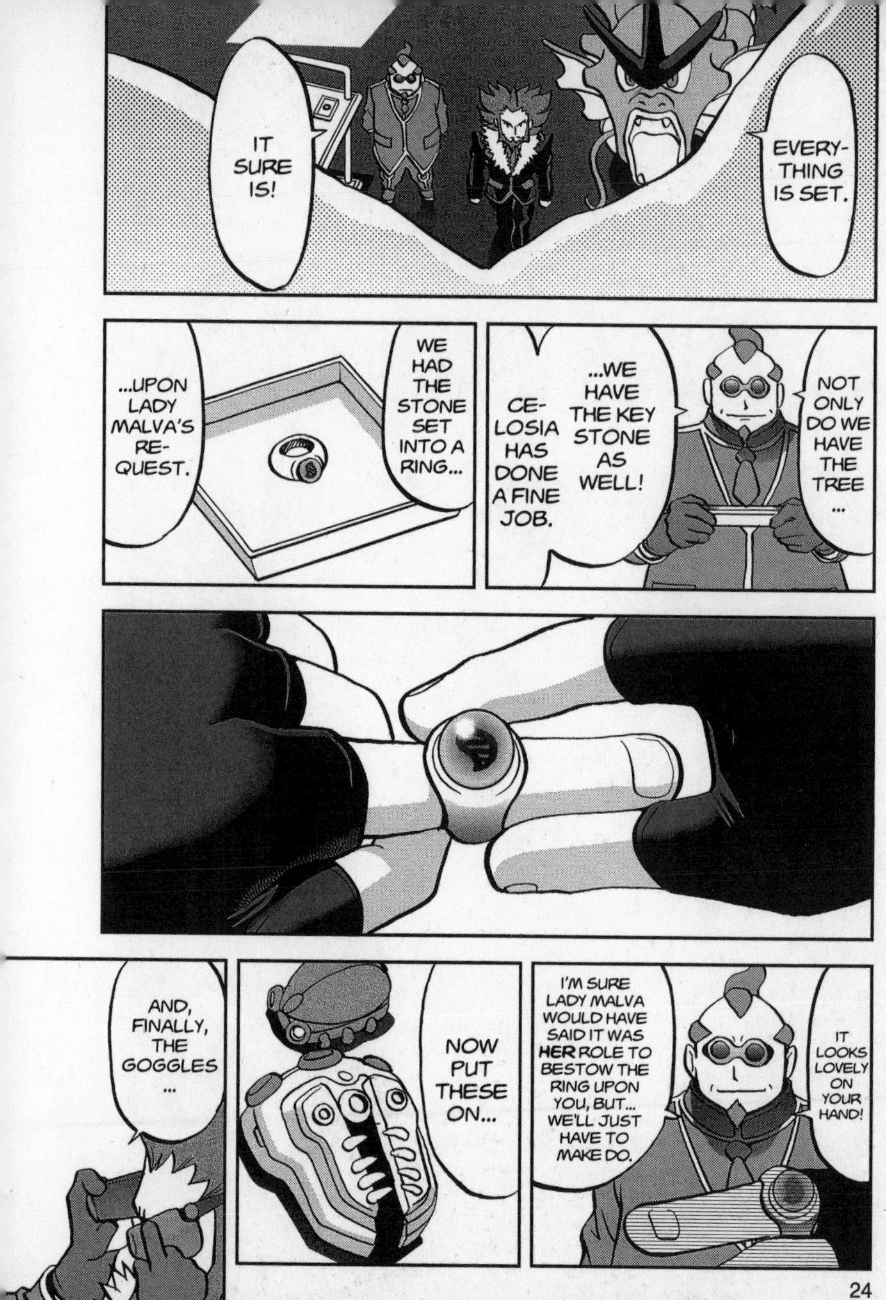
EVERYTHING IS SET.
IT SURE IS!
NOT ONLY DO WE HAVE THE TREE ...
...WE HAVE THE KEY STONE AS WELL!
CELOSIA HAS DONE A FINE JOB.
WE HAD THE STONE SET INTO A RING...
...UPON LADY MALVA'S REQUEST.
IT LOOKS LOVELY ON YOUR HAND!
I'M SURE LADY MALVA WOULD HAVE SAID IT WAS **HER** ROLE TO BESTOW THE RING UPON YOU, BUT... WE'LL JUST HAVE TO MAKE DO.
NOW PUT THESE ON...
AND, FINALLY, THE GOGGLES ...

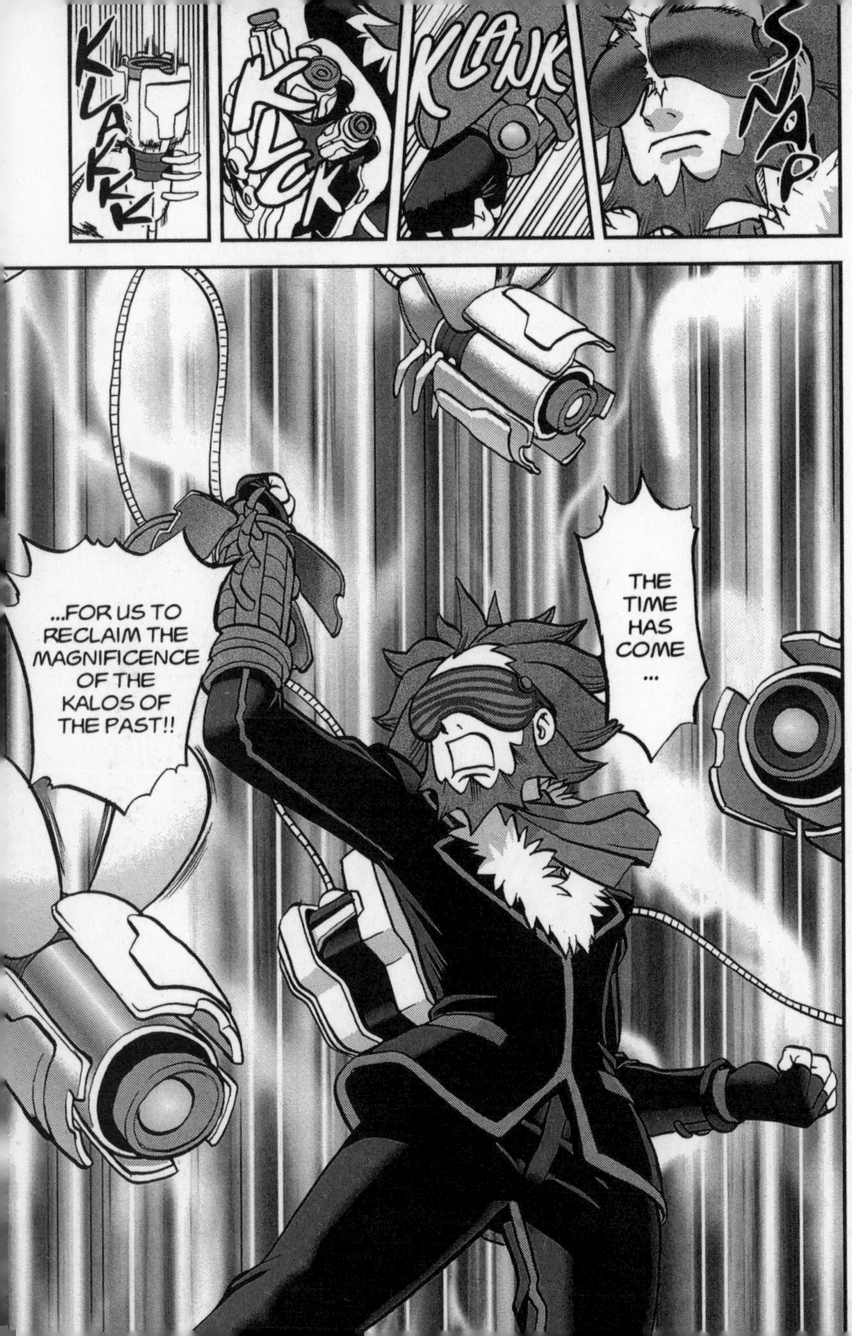
SNAP
KLANK
KLOCK
KLAKKK
THE TIME HAS COME ...
...FOR US TO RECLAIM THE MAGNIFICENCE OF THE KALOS OF THE PAST!!

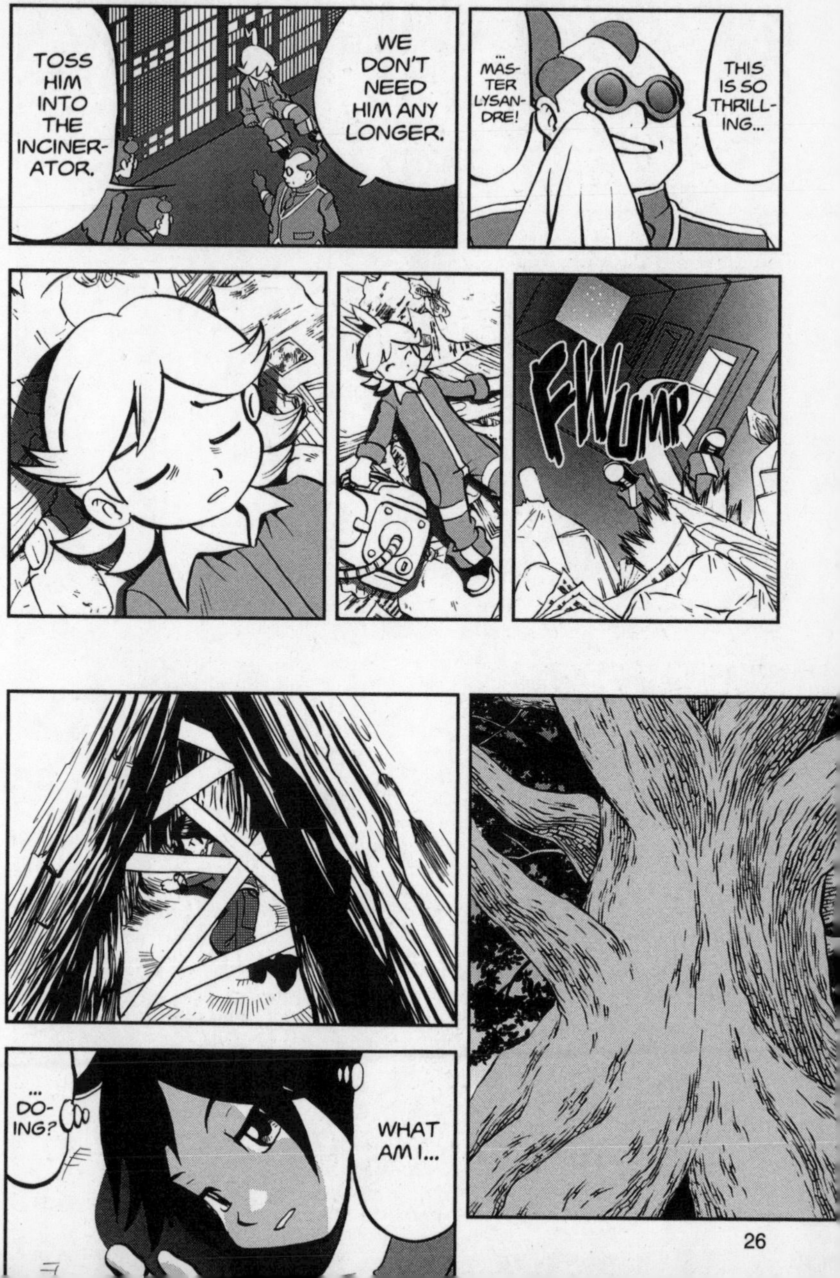
THIS IS SO THRILLING...
...MASTER LYSANDRE!
WE DON'T NEED HIM ANY LONGER.
TOSS HIM INTO THE INCINERATOR.
FWUMP
WHAT AM I...
...DOING?

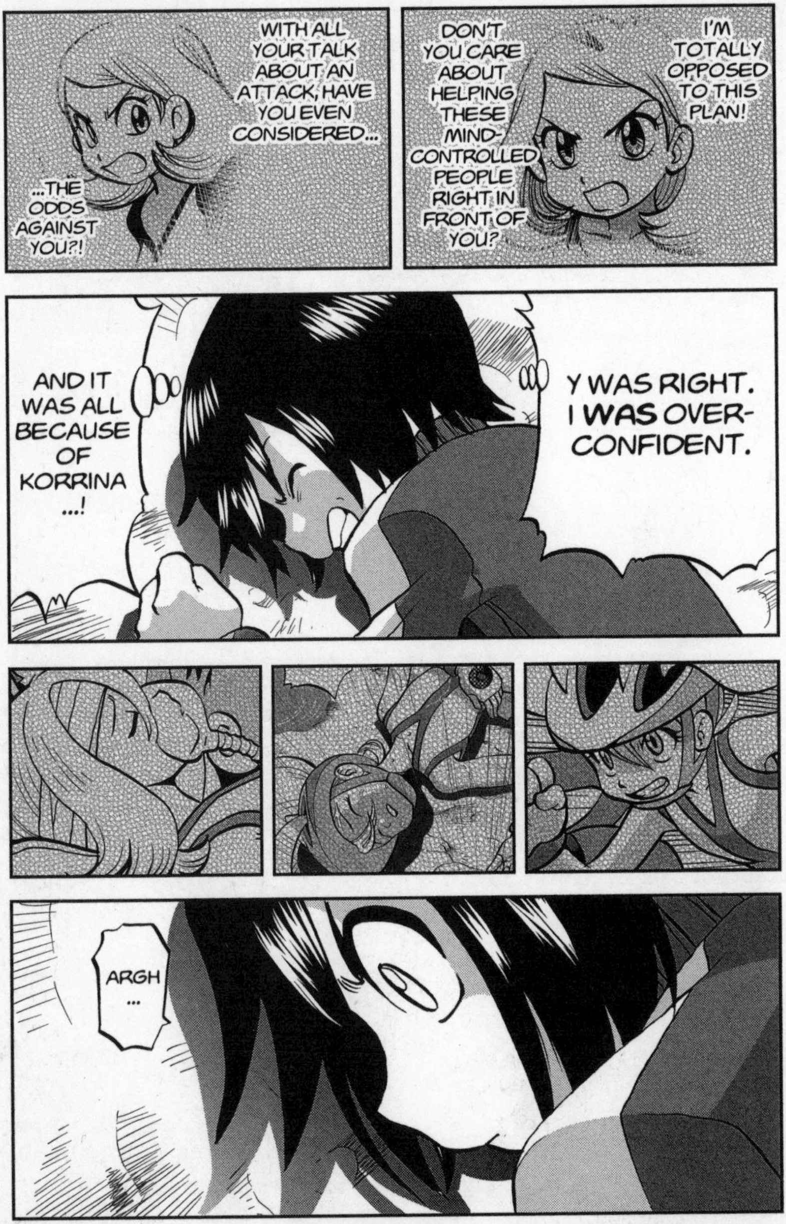
I'M TOTALLY OPPOSED TO THIS PLAN!
DON'T YOU CARE ABOUT HELPING THESE MIND-CONTROLLED PEOPLE RIGHT IN FRONT OF YOU?
WITH ALL YOUR TALK ABOUT AN ATTACK, HAVE YOU EVEN CONSIDERED...
...THE ODDS AGAINST YOU?!
Y WAS RIGHT. I **WAS** OVER-CONFIDENT.
AND IT WAS ALL BECAUSE OF KORRINA ...!
ARGH ...

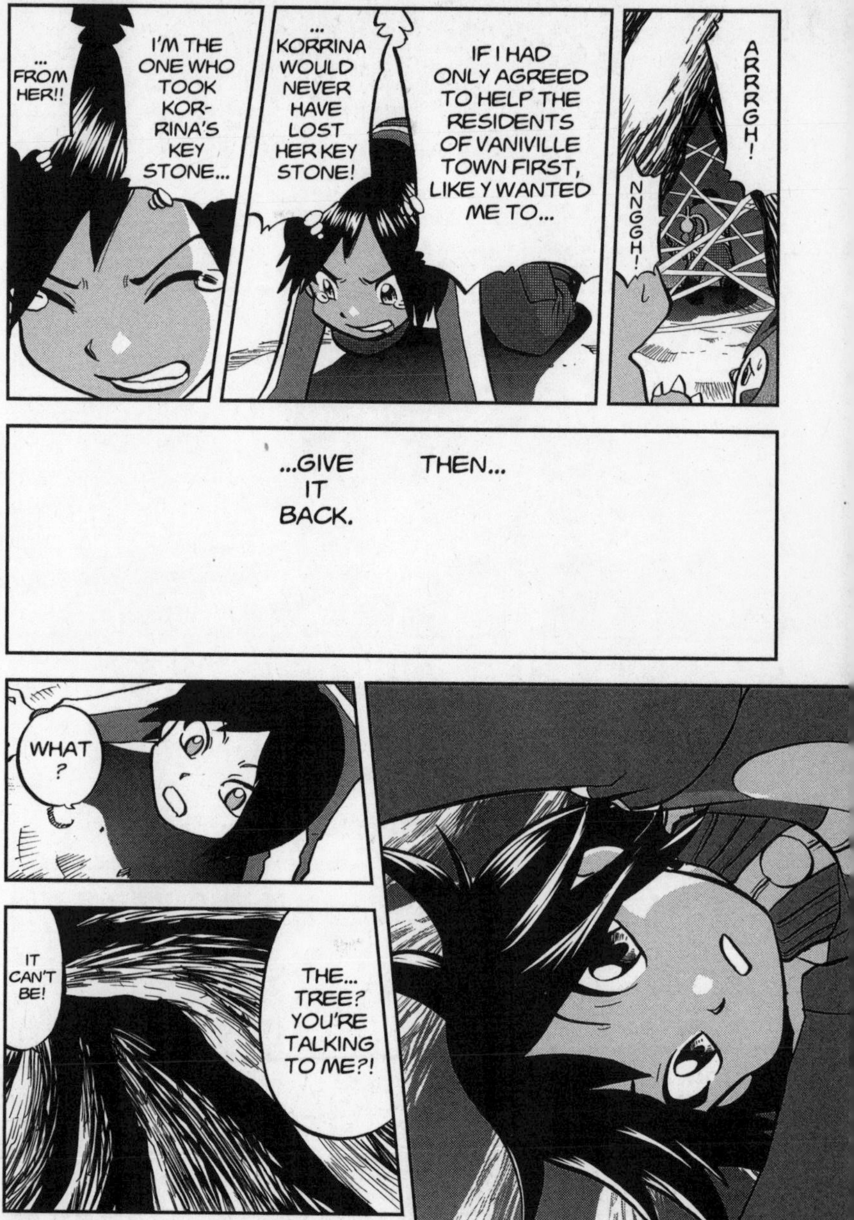
ARRRGH!
NNGGH!
IF I HAD ONLY AGREED TO HELP THE RESIDENTS OF VANIVILLE TOWN FIRST, LIKE Y WANTED ME TO...
... KORRINA WOULD NEVER HAVE LOST HER KEY STONE!
I'M THE ONE WHO TOOK KOR-RINA'S KEY STONE...
... FROM HER!!
THEN...
...GIVE IT BACK.
WHAT?
THE... TREE? YOU'RE TALKING TO ME?!
IT CAN'T BE!

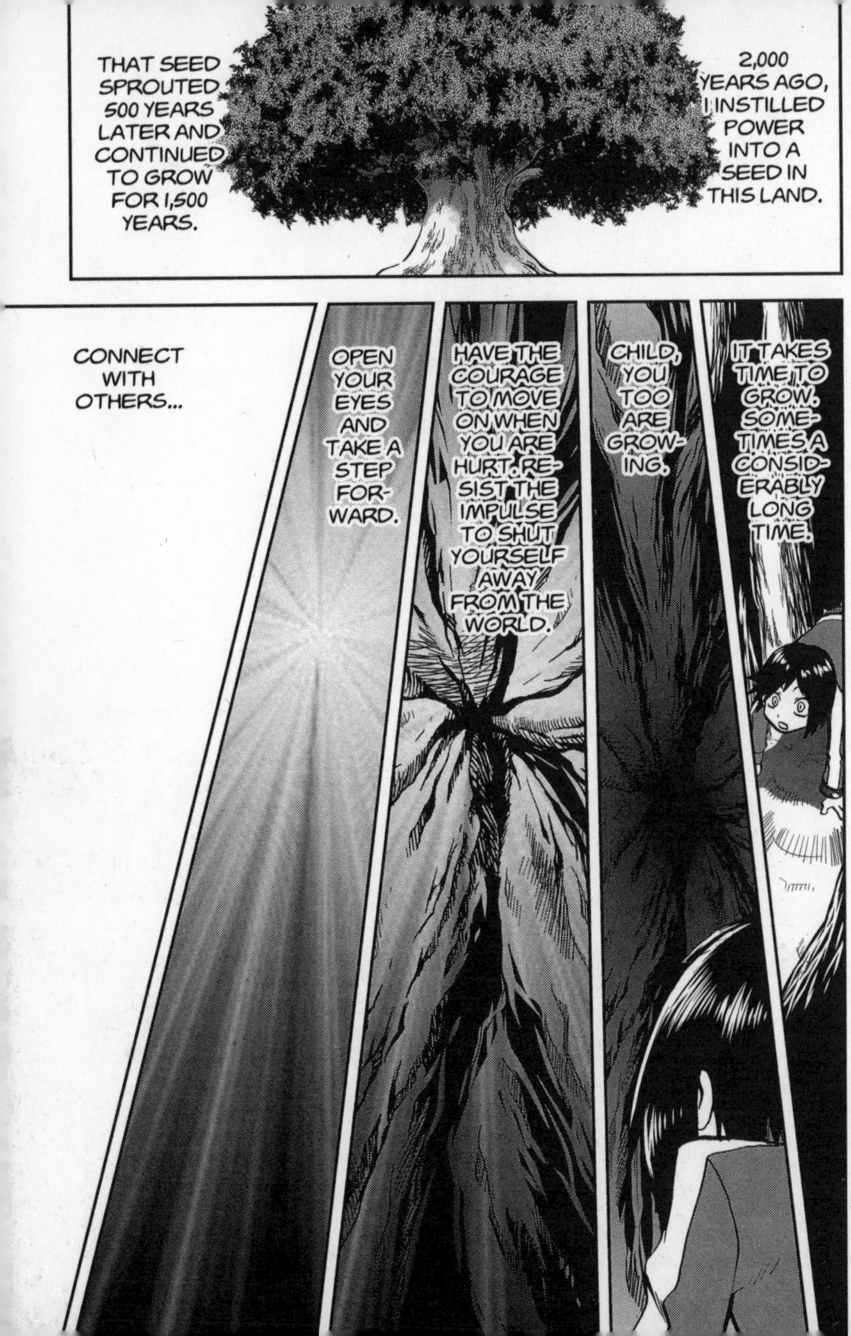
2,000 YEARS AGO, I INSTILLED POWER INTO A SEED IN THIS LAND.
THAT SEED SPROUTED 500 YEARS LATER AND CONTINUED TO GROW FOR 1,500 YEARS.
IT TAKES TIME TO GROW. SOMETIMES A CONSIDERABLY LONG TIME.
CHILD, YOU TOO ARE GROWING.
HAVE THE COURAGE TO MOVE ON WHEN YOU ARE HURT. RESIST THE IMPULSE TO SHUT YOURSELF AWAY FROM THE WORLD.
OPEN YOUR EYES AND TAKE A STEP FORWARD.
CONNECT WITH OTHERS...

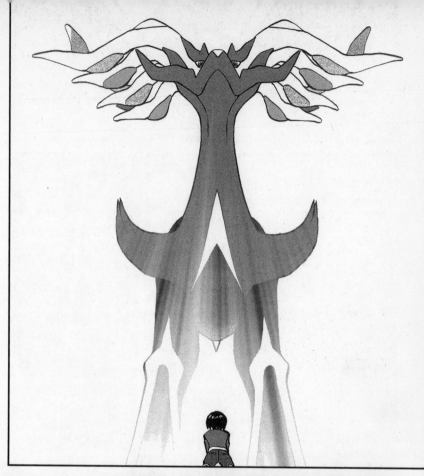

HUH ?

THANK YOU, KLEFKI. I'M BETTER NOW...

PAT

PAT

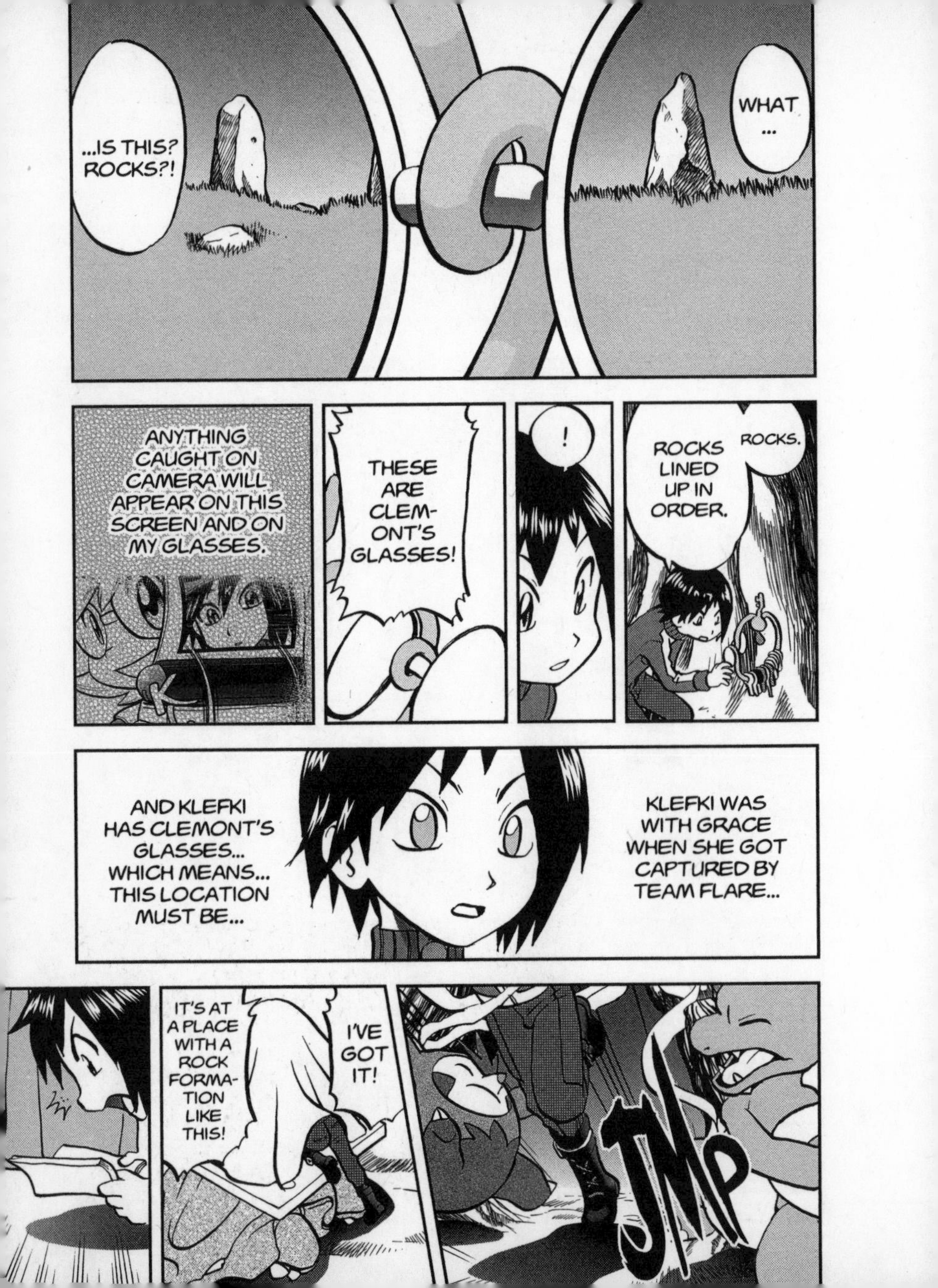
WHAT ...
...IS THIS? ROCKS?!
ROCKS.
ROCKS LINED UP IN ORDER.
!
THESE ARE CLEM-ONT'S GLASSES!
ANYTHING CAUGHT ON CAMERA WILL APPEAR ON THIS SCREEN AND ON MY GLASSES.
KLEFKI WAS WITH GRACE WHEN SHE GOT CAPTURED BY TEAM FLARE...
AND KLEFKI HAS CLEMONT'S GLASSES... WHICH MEANS... THIS LOCATION MUST BE...
JMP
I'VE GOT IT!
IT'S AT A PLACE WITH A ROCK FORMA-TION LIKE THIS!

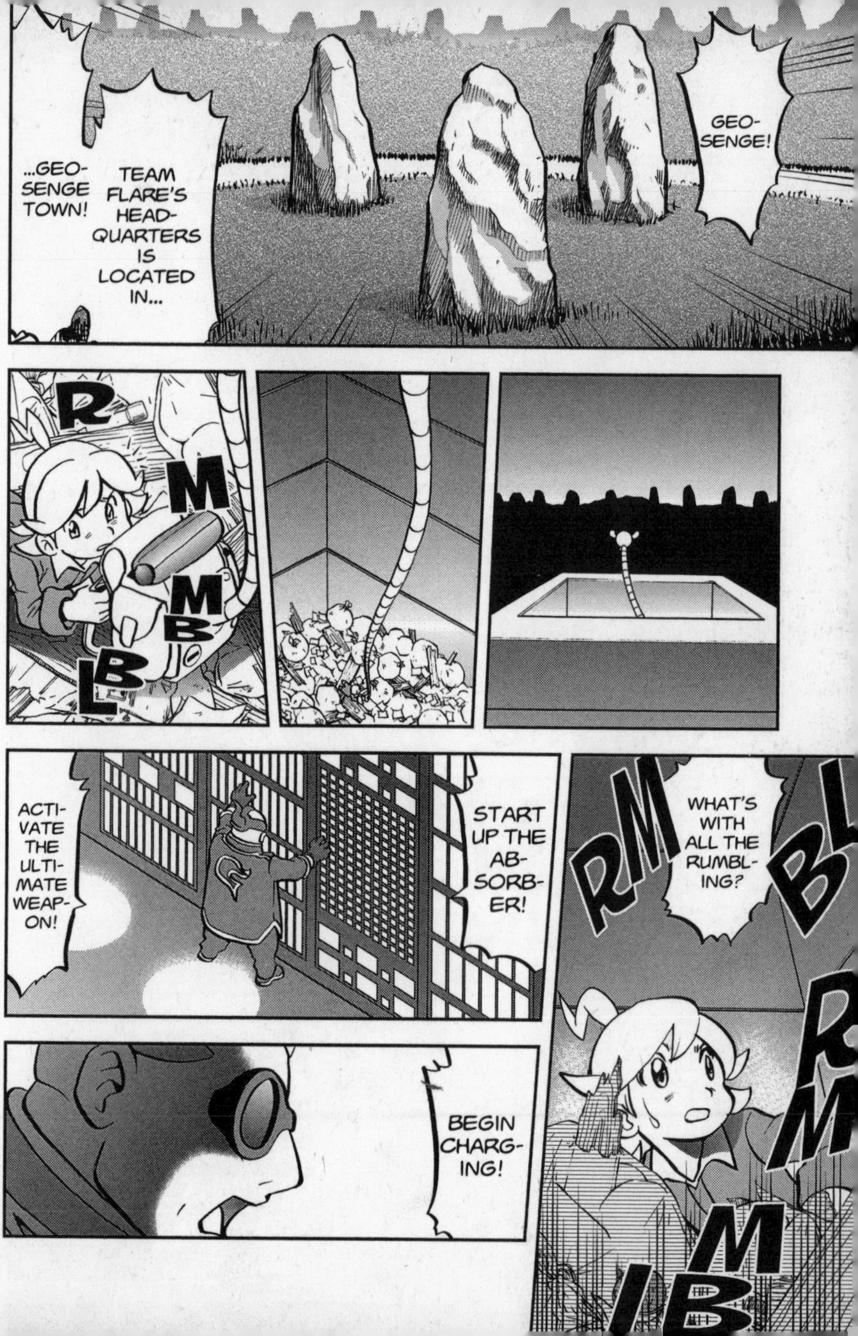
GEO-SENGE!
TEAM FLARE'S HEAD-QUARTERS IS LOCATED IN...
...GEO-SENGE TOWN!
RMMBBL
RMBL
WHAT'S WITH ALL THE RUMBL-ING?
START UP THE AB-SORB-ER!
ACTI-VATE THE ULTI-MATE WEAP-ON!
BEGIN CHARG-ING!

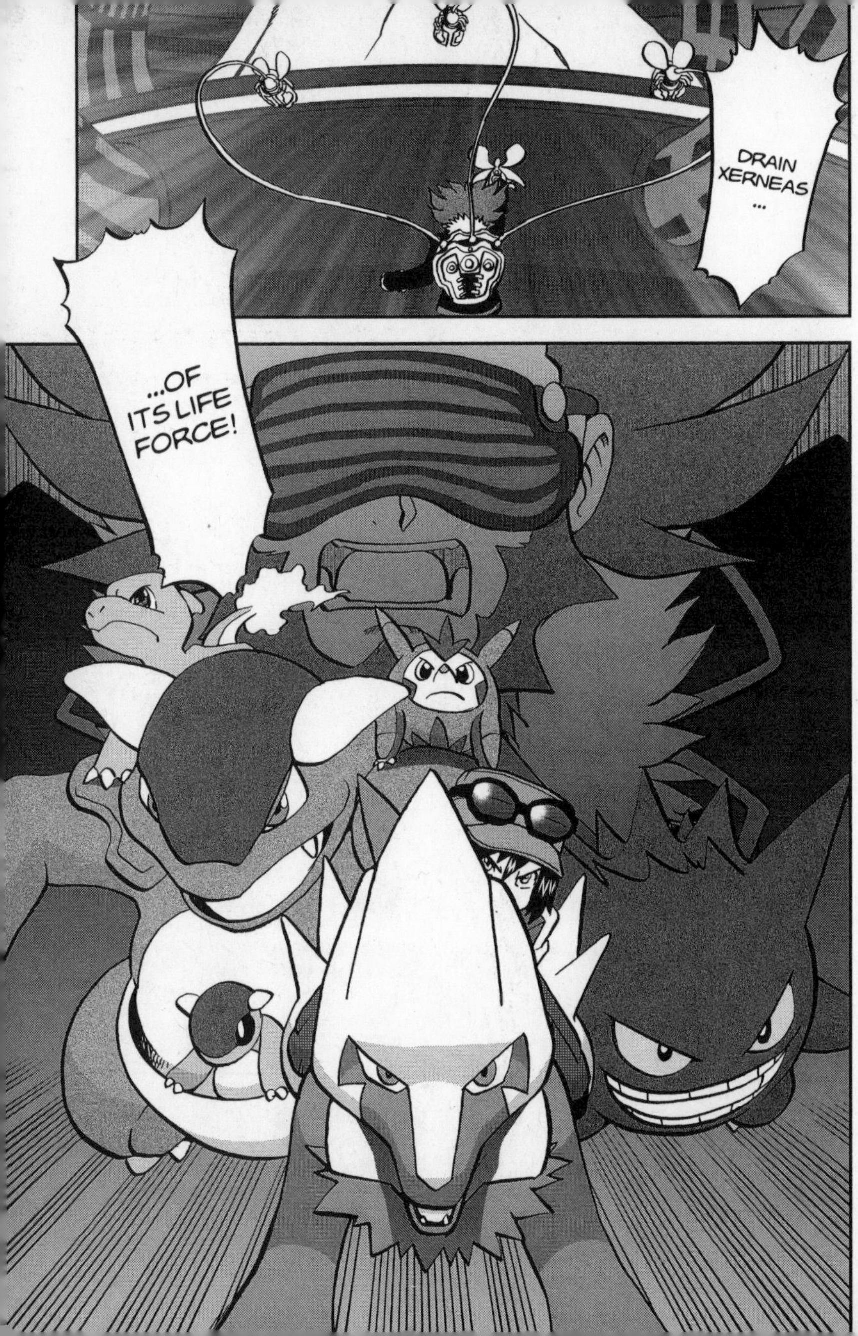
DRAIN XERNEAS ...
...OF ITS LIFE FORCE!

Current Location

Laverre City

An unearthly city created by those inspired by a mysterious and ancient tree 1,500 years old.

**Route 12
Fourrage Road**

Frolicking Skiddo can be seen and ridden at the Baa de Mer Ranch, located beside the breezy sea.

Adventure 23 Gyarados Changes

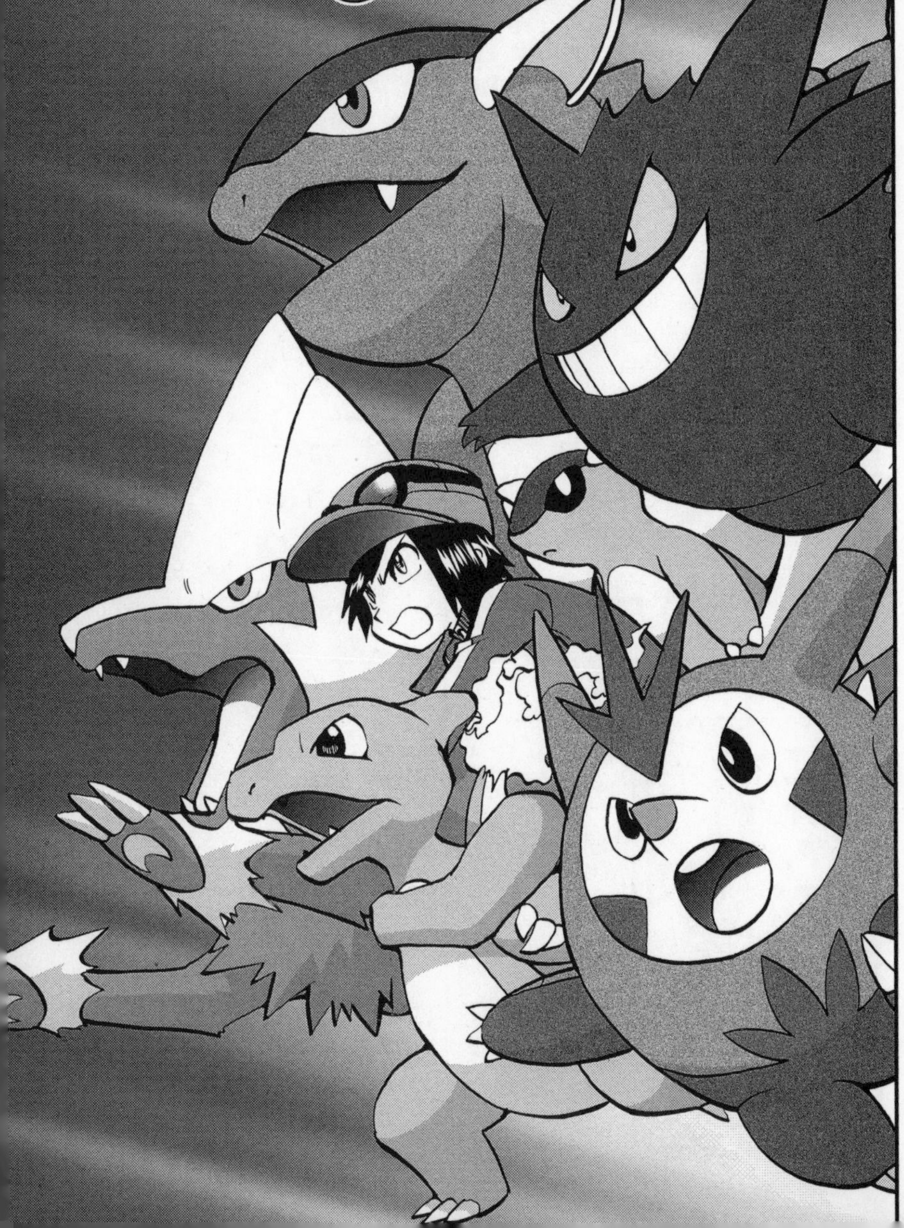

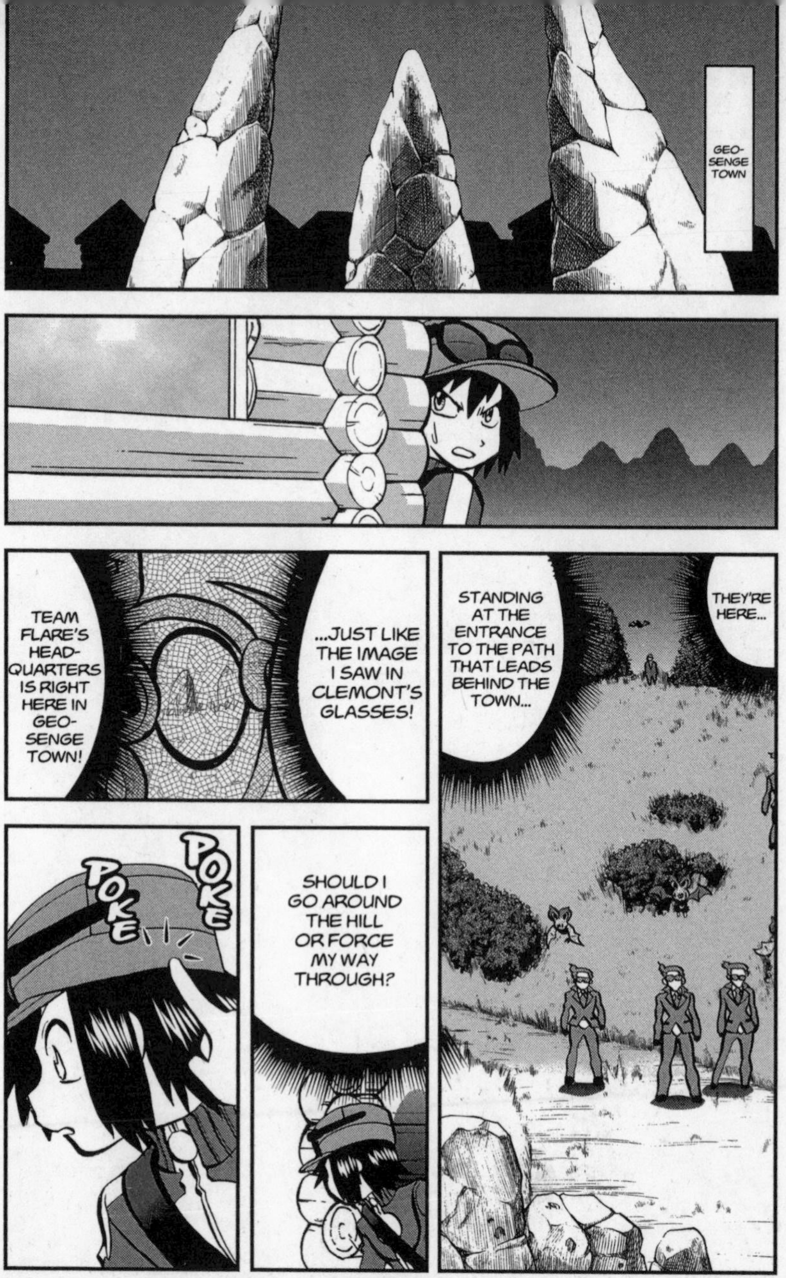
GEO-SENGE TOWN
THEY'RE HERE...
STANDING AT THE ENTRANCE TO THE PATH THAT LEADS BEHIND THE TOWN...
...JUST LIKE THE IMAGE I SAW IN CLEMONT'S GLASSES!
TEAM FLARE'S HEAD-QUARTERS IS RIGHT HERE IN GEO-SENGE TOWN!
SHOULD I GO AROUND THE HILL OR FORCE MY WAY THROUGH?
POKE
POKE

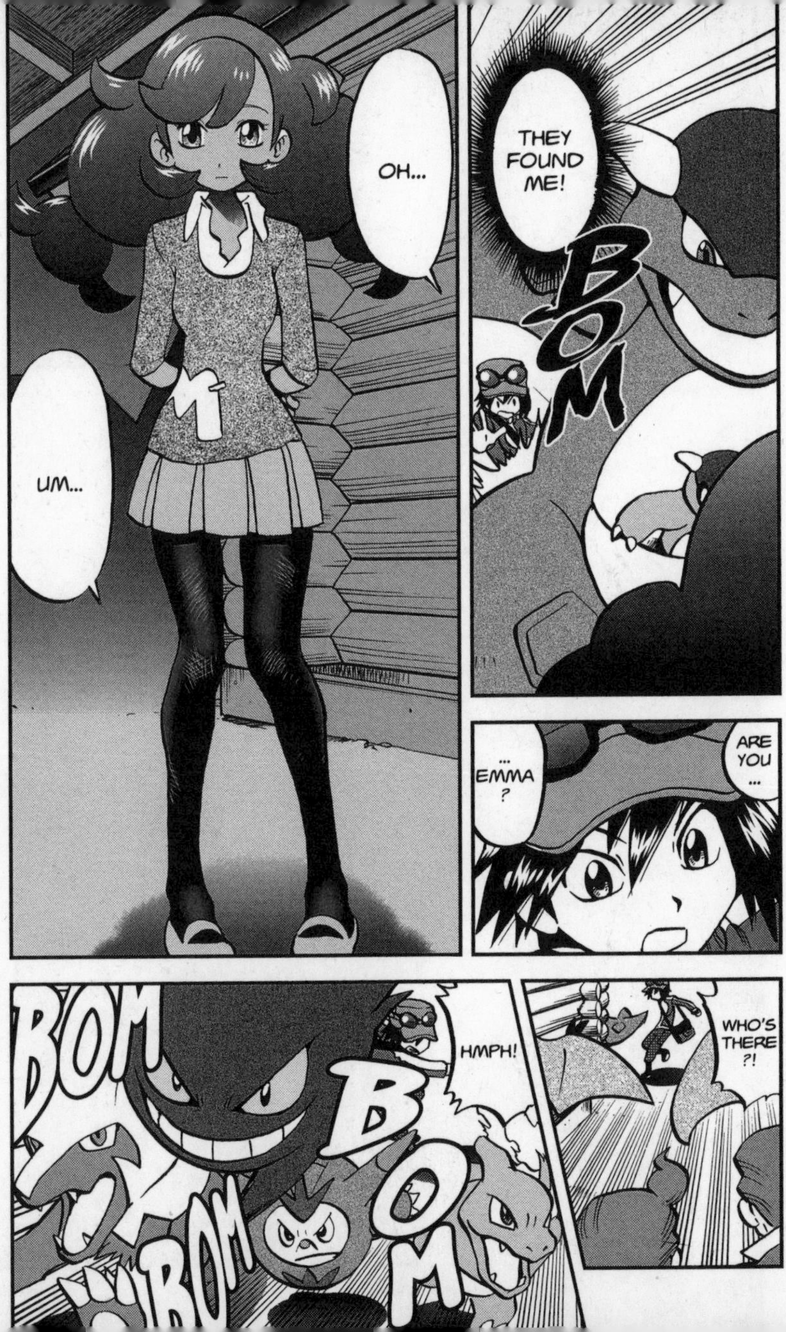
THEY FOUND ME!
BOM
ARE YOU ...
... EMMA ?
OH...
UM...
WHO'S THERE ?!
HMPH!
BOM
BOM
BOM
BOM

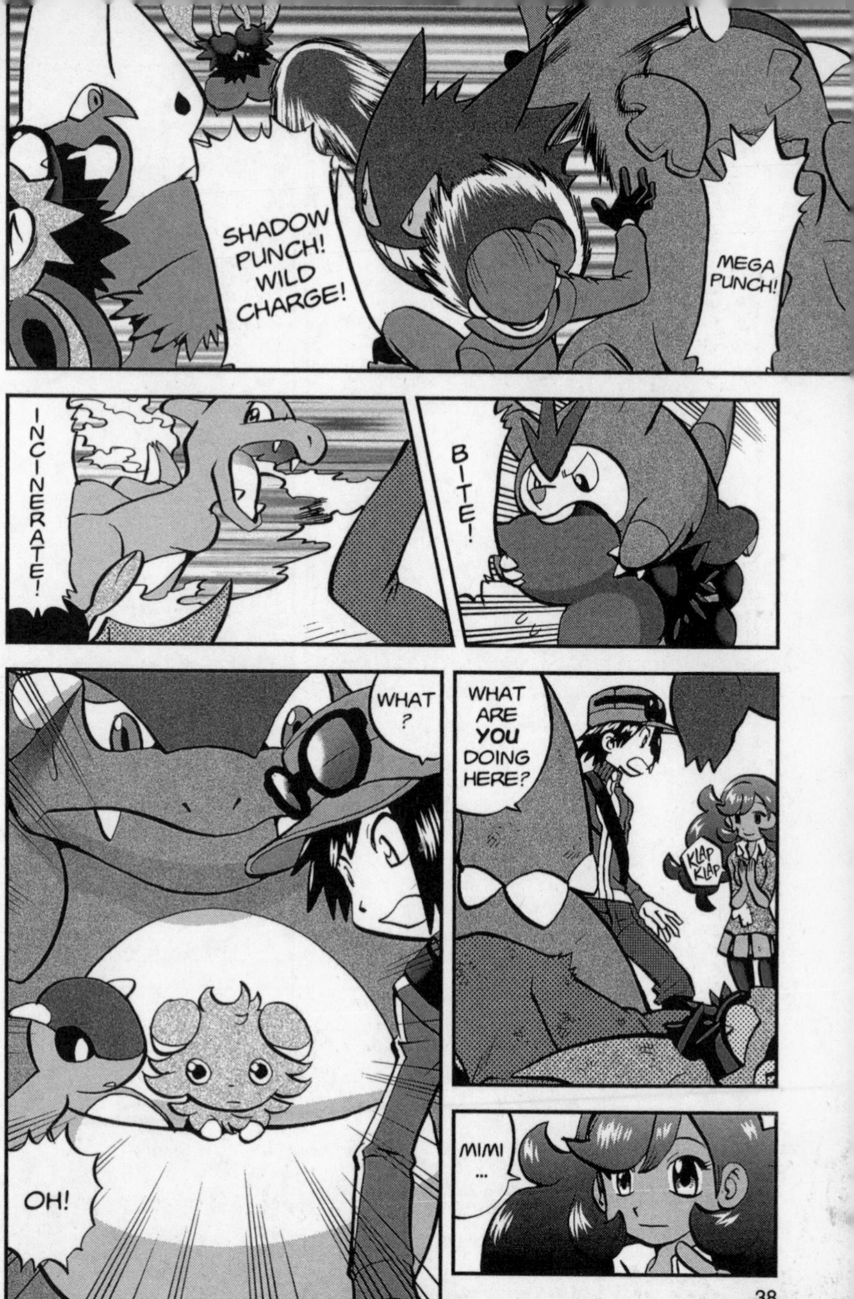
MEGA PUNCH!
SHADOW PUNCH! WILD CHARGE!
BITE!
INCINERATE!
WHAT ARE **YOU** DOING HERE?
KLAP KLAP
MIMI ...
WHAT ?
OH!

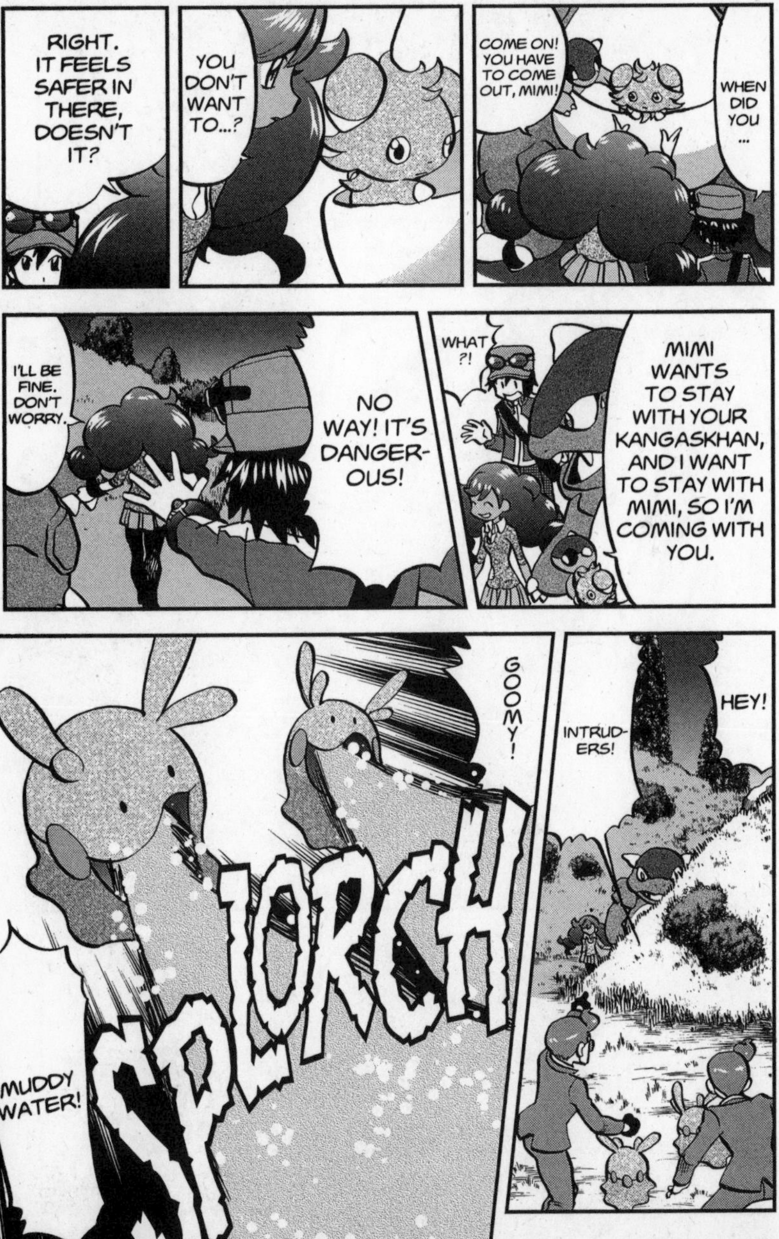
WHEN DID YOU ...
COME ON! YOU HAVE TO COME OUT, MIMI!
YOU DON'T WANT TO...?
RIGHT. IT FEELS SAFER IN THERE, DOESN'T IT?
MIMI WANTS TO STAY WITH YOUR KANGASKHAN, AND I WANT TO STAY WITH MIMI, SO I'M COMING WITH YOU.
WHAT?!
NO WAY! IT'S DANGER-OUS!
I'LL BE FINE. DON'T WORRY.
HEY!
INTRUD-ERS!
GOOOMY!
SPLORCH
MUDDY WATER!

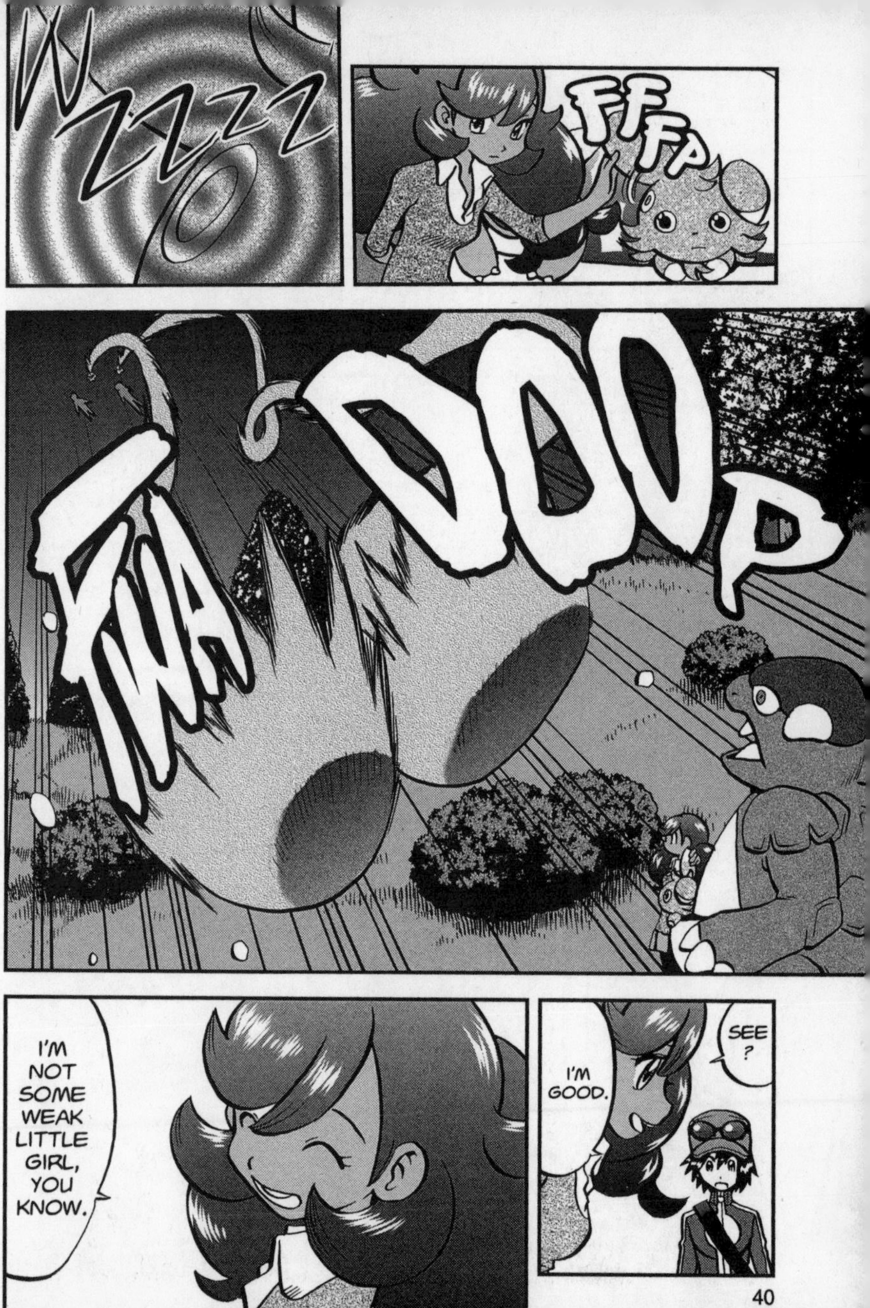
FFFP
WZZZZZ
FWADOOP
SEE?
I'M GOOD.
I'M NOT SOME WEAK LITTLE GIRL, YOU KNOW.

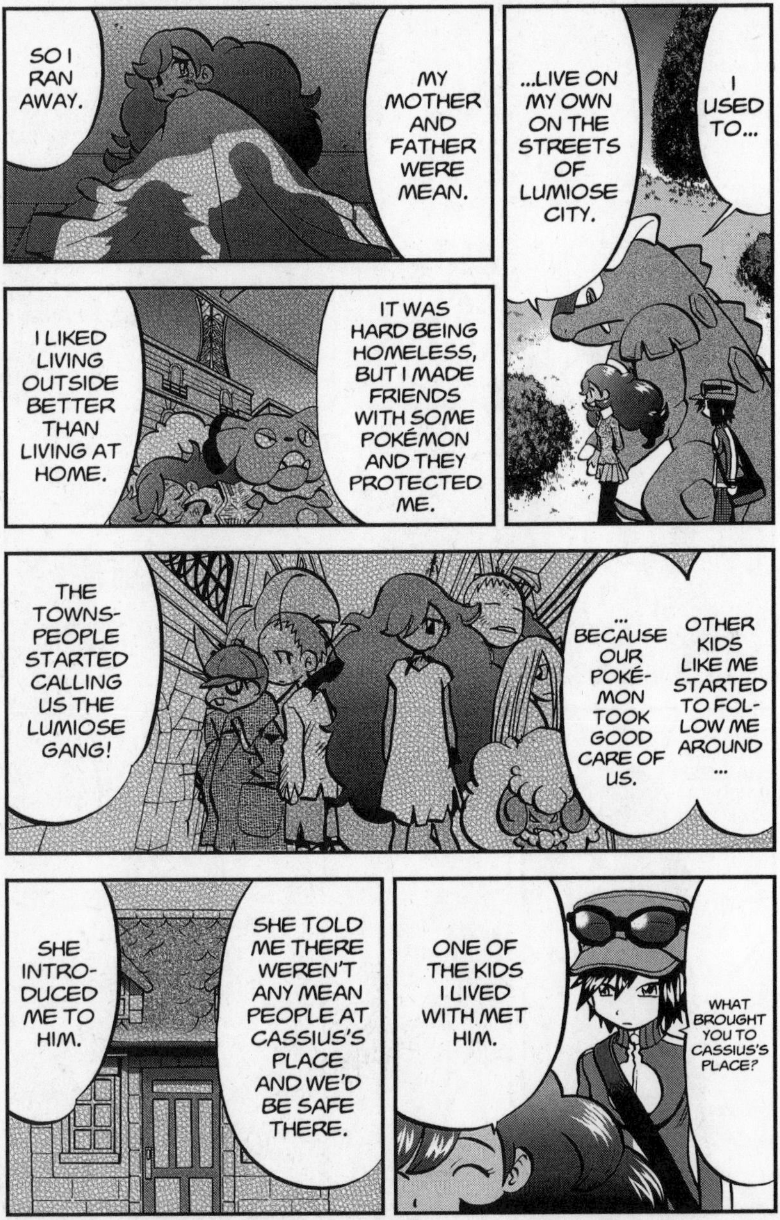
I USED TO...
...LIVE ON MY OWN ON THE STREETS OF LUMIOSE CITY.
MY MOTHER AND FATHER WERE MEAN.
SO I RAN AWAY.
IT WAS HARD BEING HOMELESS, BUT I MADE FRIENDS WITH SOME POKÉMON AND THEY PROTECTED ME.
I LIKED LIVING OUTSIDE BETTER THAN LIVING AT HOME.
OTHER KIDS LIKE ME STARTED TO FOL-LOW ME AROUND...
...BECAUSE OUR POKÉ-MON TOOK GOOD CARE OF US.
THE TOWNS-PEOPLE STARTED CALLING US THE LUMIOSE GANG!
WHAT BROUGHT YOU TO CASSIUS'S PLACE?
ONE OF THE KIDS I LIVED WITH MET HIM.
SHE TOLD ME THERE WEREN'T ANY MEAN PEOPLE AT CASSIUS'S PLACE AND WE'D BE SAFE THERE.
SHE INTRO-DUCED ME TO HIM.

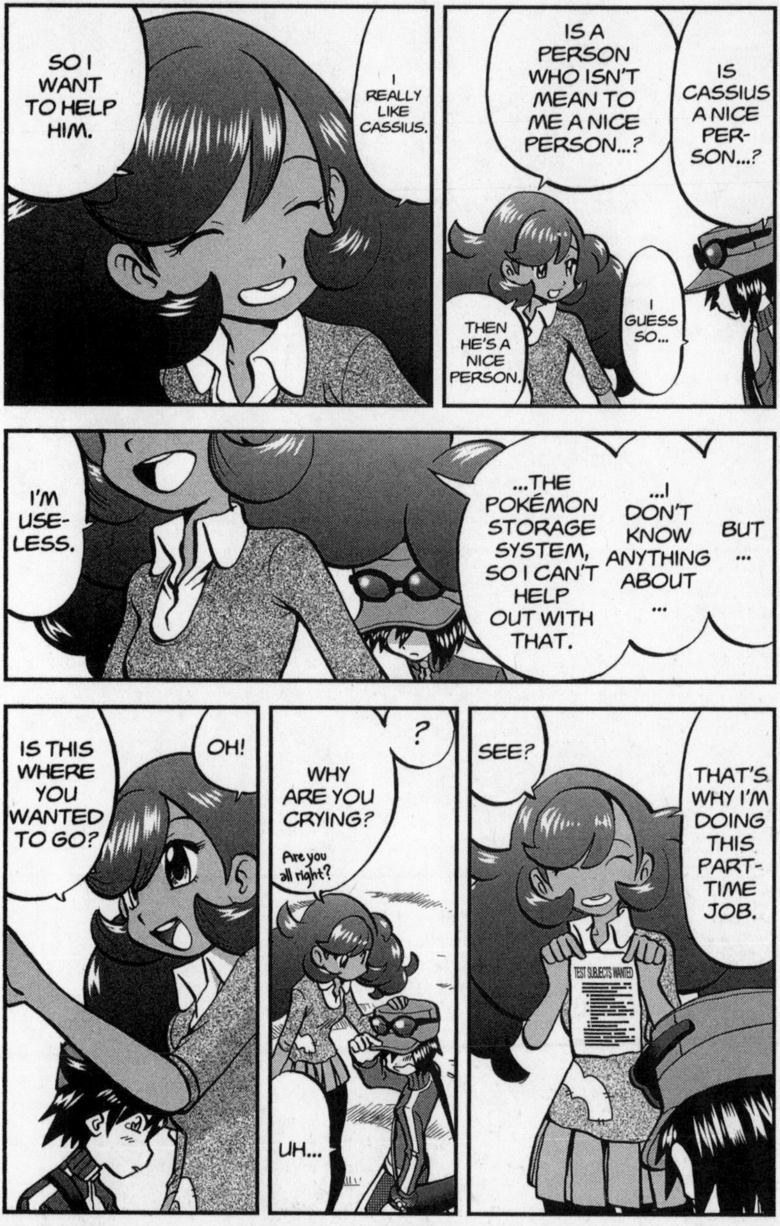

IS CASSIUS A NICE PERSON...?
IS A PERSON WHO ISN'T MEAN TO ME A NICE PERSON...?
I GUESS SO...
THEN HE'S A NICE PERSON.
I REALLY LIKE CASSIUS.
SO I WANT TO HELP HIM.
BUT...
...I DON'T KNOW ANYTHING ABOUT...
...THE POKÉMON STORAGE SYSTEM, SO I CAN'T HELP OUT WITH THAT.
I'M USELESS.
THAT'S WHY I'M DOING THIS PART-TIME JOB.
SEE?
TEST SUBJECTS WANTED
?
WHY ARE YOU CRYING?
Are you all right?
UH...
OH!
IS THIS WHERE YOU WANTED TO GO?

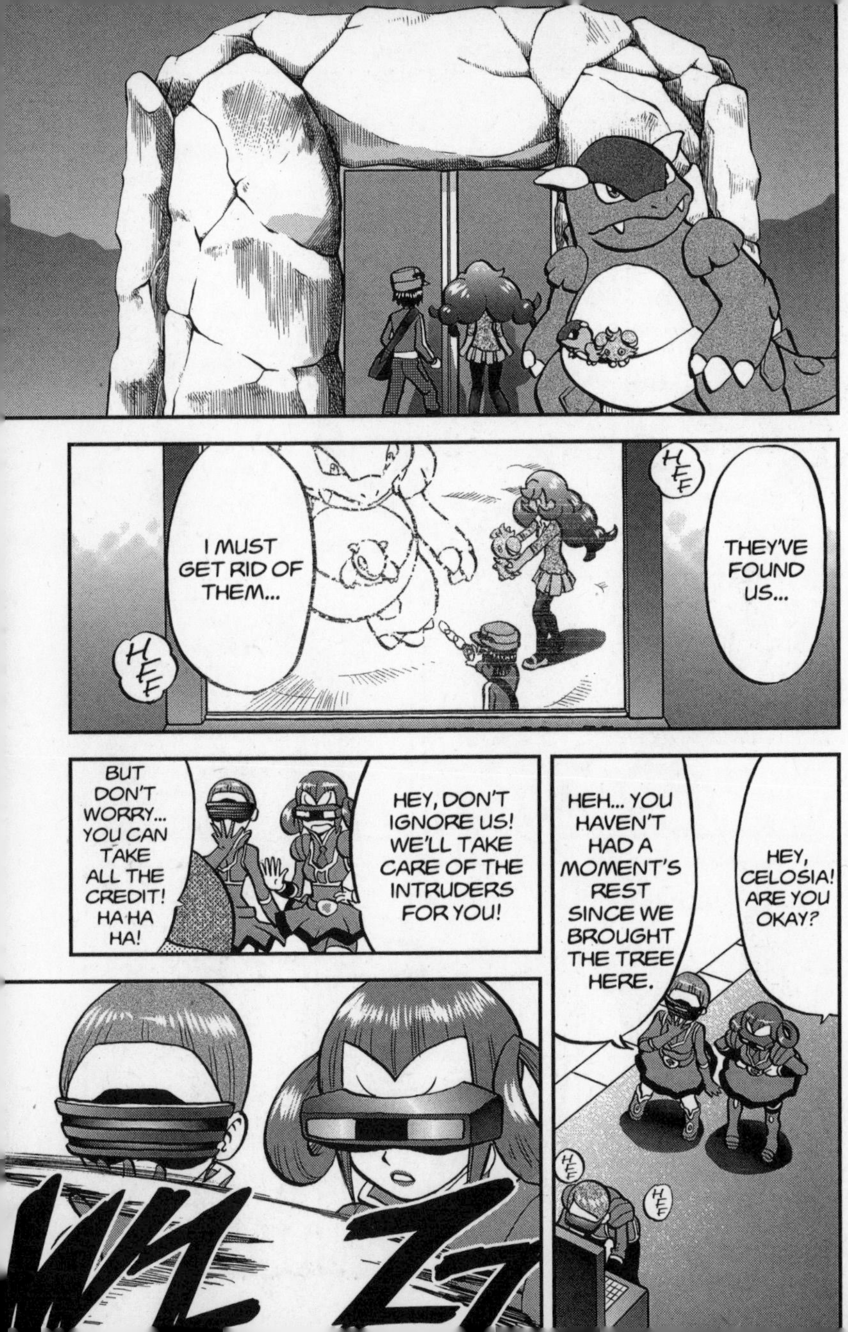
HEE
THEY'VE FOUND US...
I MUST GET RID OF THEM...
HEE
HEY, CELOSIA! ARE YOU OKAY?
HEH... YOU HAVEN'T HAD A MOMENT'S REST SINCE WE BROUGHT THE TREE HERE.
HEE
HEE
HEY, DON'T IGNORE US! WE'LL TAKE CARE OF THE INTRUDERS FOR YOU!
BUT DON'T WORRY... YOU CAN TAKE ALL THE CREDIT! HA HA HA HA!

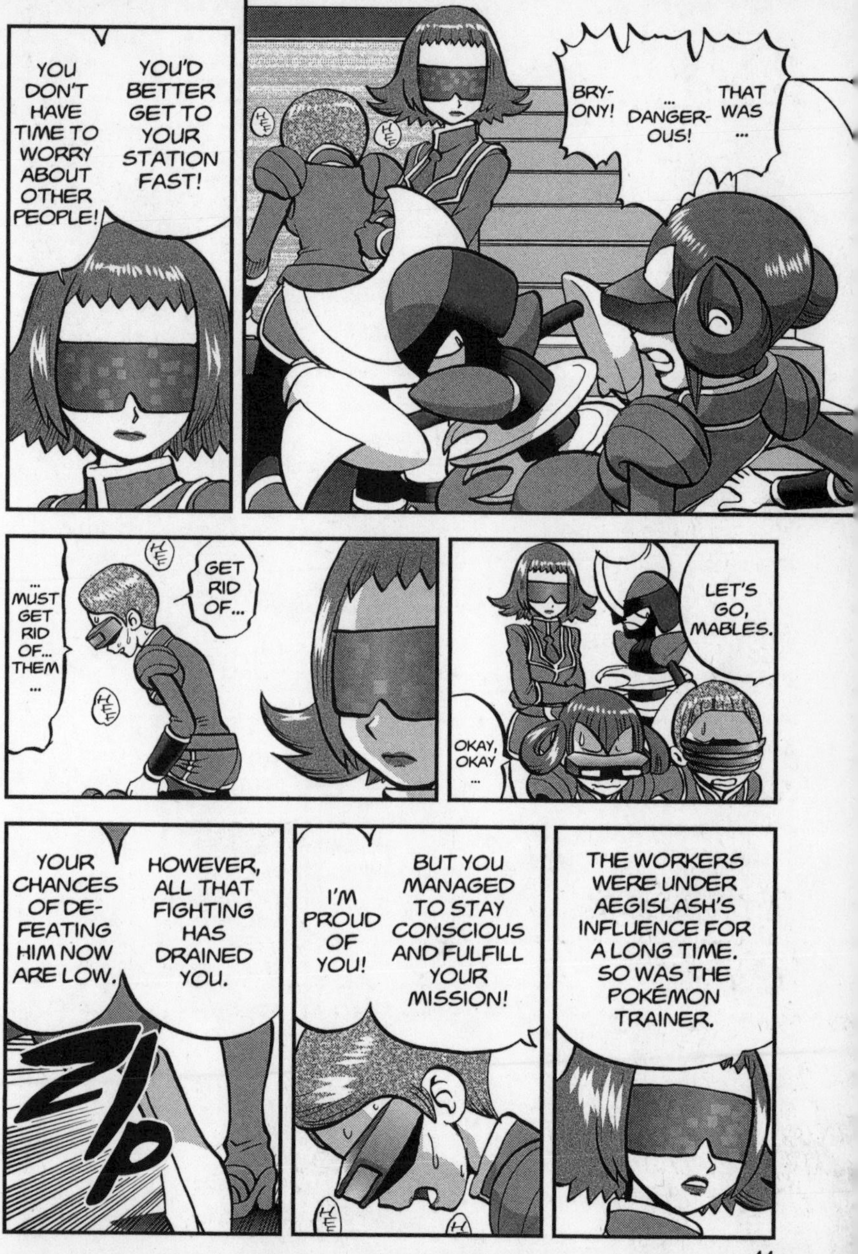
THAT WAS ... ... DANGEROUS! BRYONY!
HEF
HEF
YOU'D BETTER GET TO YOUR STATION FAST!
YOU DON'T HAVE TIME TO WORRY ABOUT OTHER PEOPLE!
LET'S GO, MABLES.
OKAY, OKAY ...
HEF
GET RID OF...
... MUST GET RID OF... THEM ...
HEF
THE WORKERS WERE UNDER AEGISLASH'S INFLUENCE FOR A LONG TIME. SO WAS THE POKÉMON TRAINER.
BUT YOU MANAGED TO STAY CONSCIOUS AND FULFILL YOUR MISSION!
I'M PROUD OF YOU!
HEF
HEF
HOWEVER, ALL THAT FIGHTING HAS DRAINED YOU.
YOUR CHANCES OF DEFEATING HIM NOW ARE LOW.
ZIP

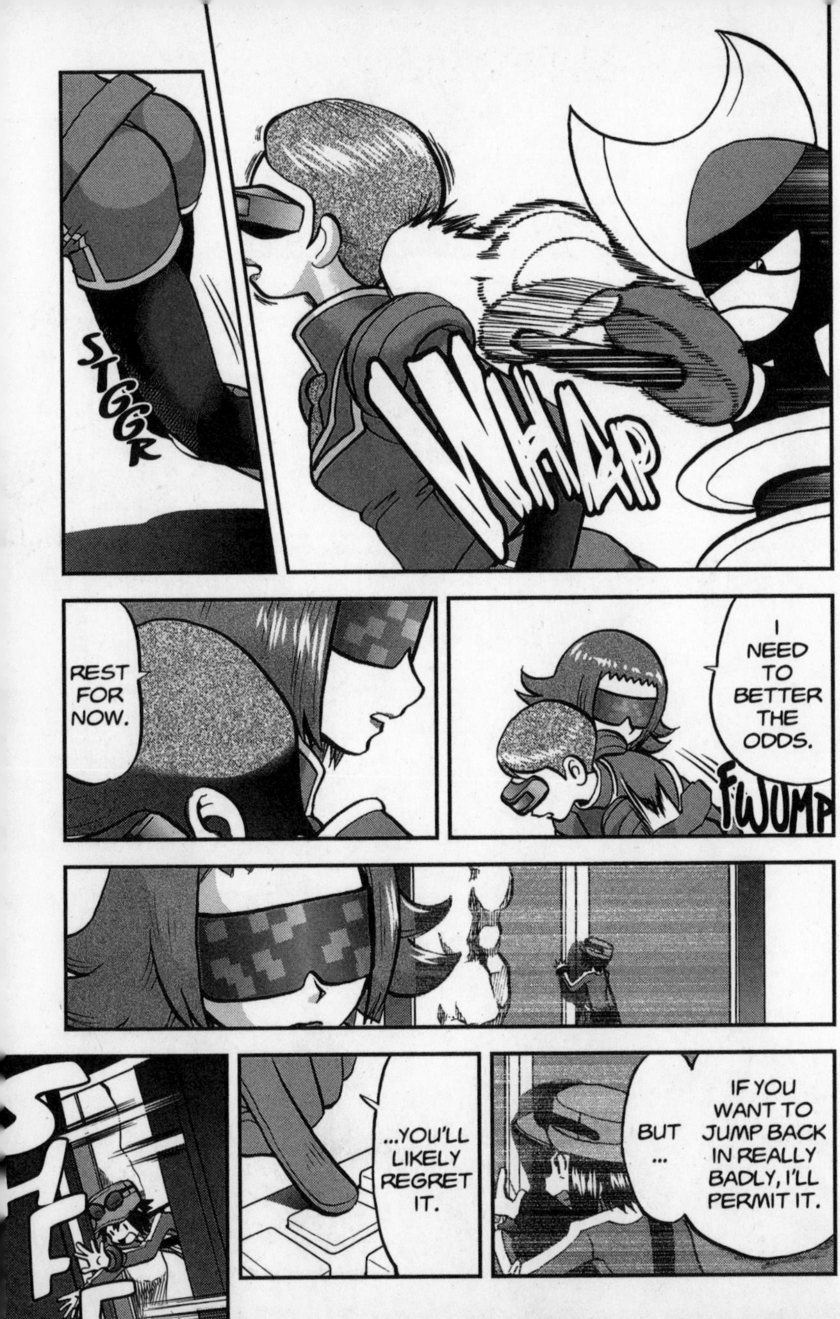
WHAP
STGGR
I NEED TO BETTER THE ODDS.
FWUMP
REST FOR NOW.
IF YOU WANT TO JUMP BACK IN REALLY BADLY, I'LL PERMIT IT.
BUT ...
...YOU'LL LIKELY REGRET IT.

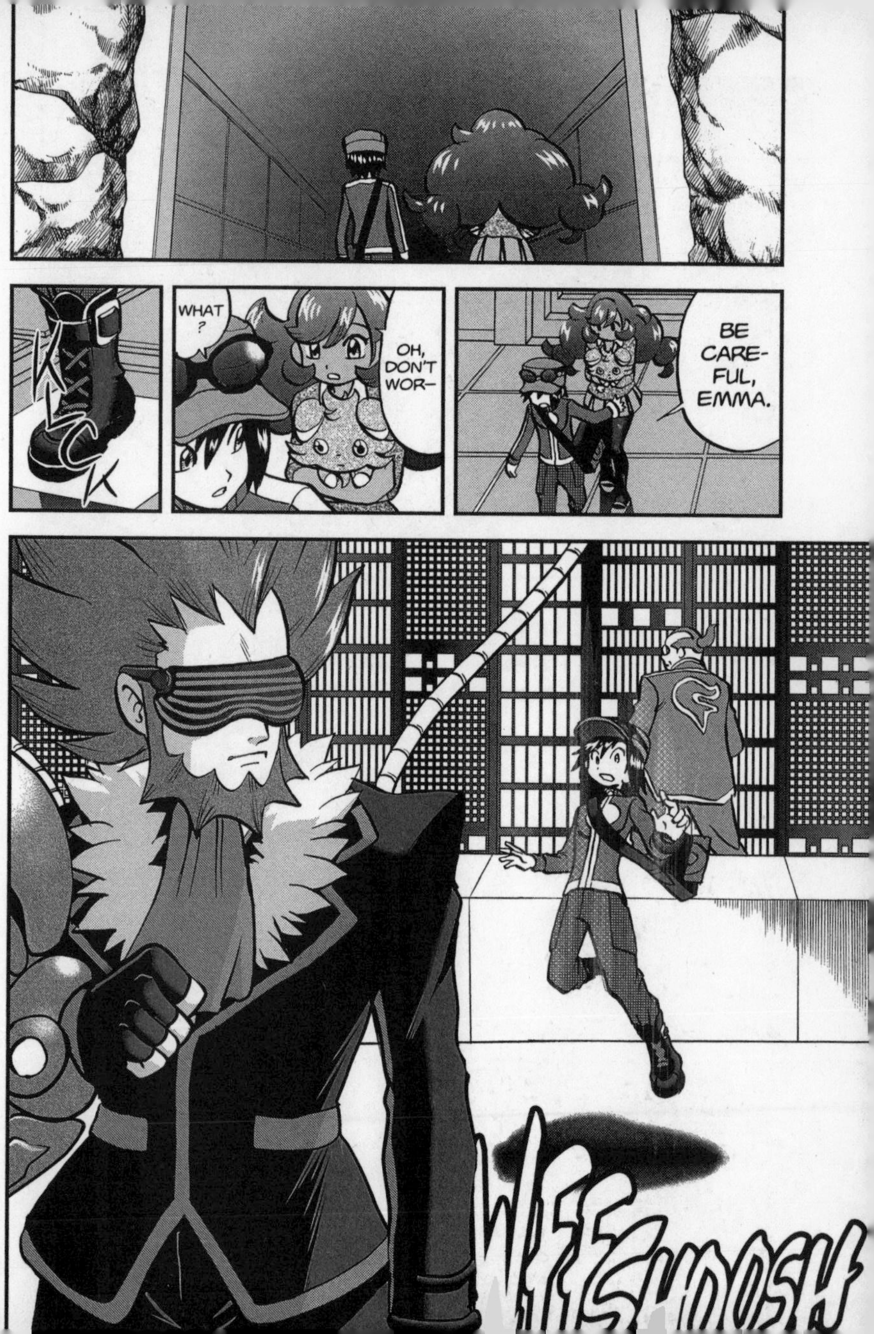
BE CAREFUL, EMMA.
WHAT?
OH, DON'T WOR—
KLCK
SHOOSH

YOU MANAGED TO COME TO ME ALL BY YOURSELF...

HM...

...ARE A CHOSEN ONE.

YOU TOO...

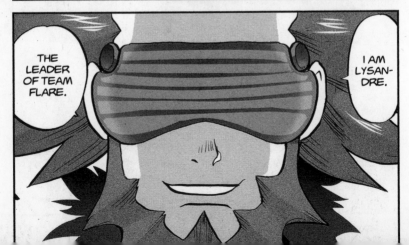

THE LEADER OF TEAM FLARE.

I AM LYSAN- DRE.

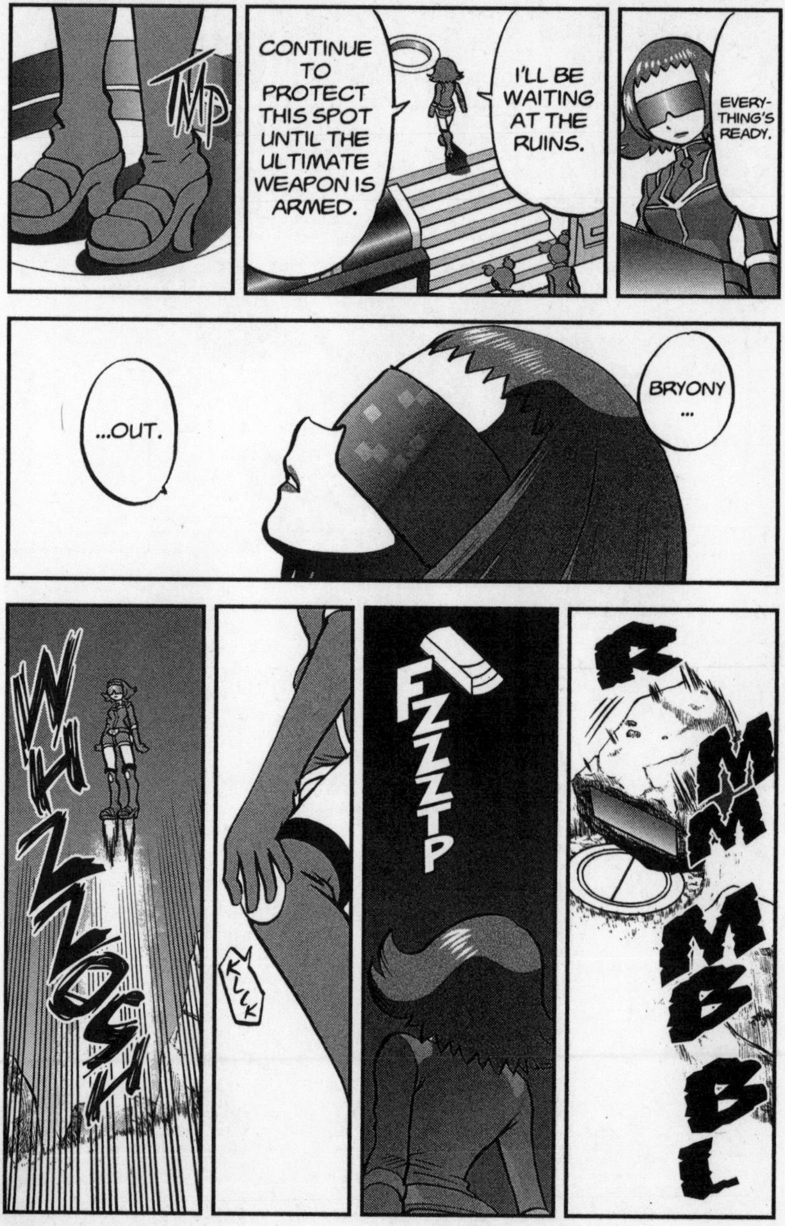
EVERYTHING'S READY.
I'LL BE WAITING AT THE RUINS.
CONTINUE TO PROTECT THIS SPOT UNTIL THE ULTIMATE WEAPON IS ARMED.
TMP
BRYONY...
...OUT.
RMMMBBL
FZZZTP
KLIK
WHZZOSH

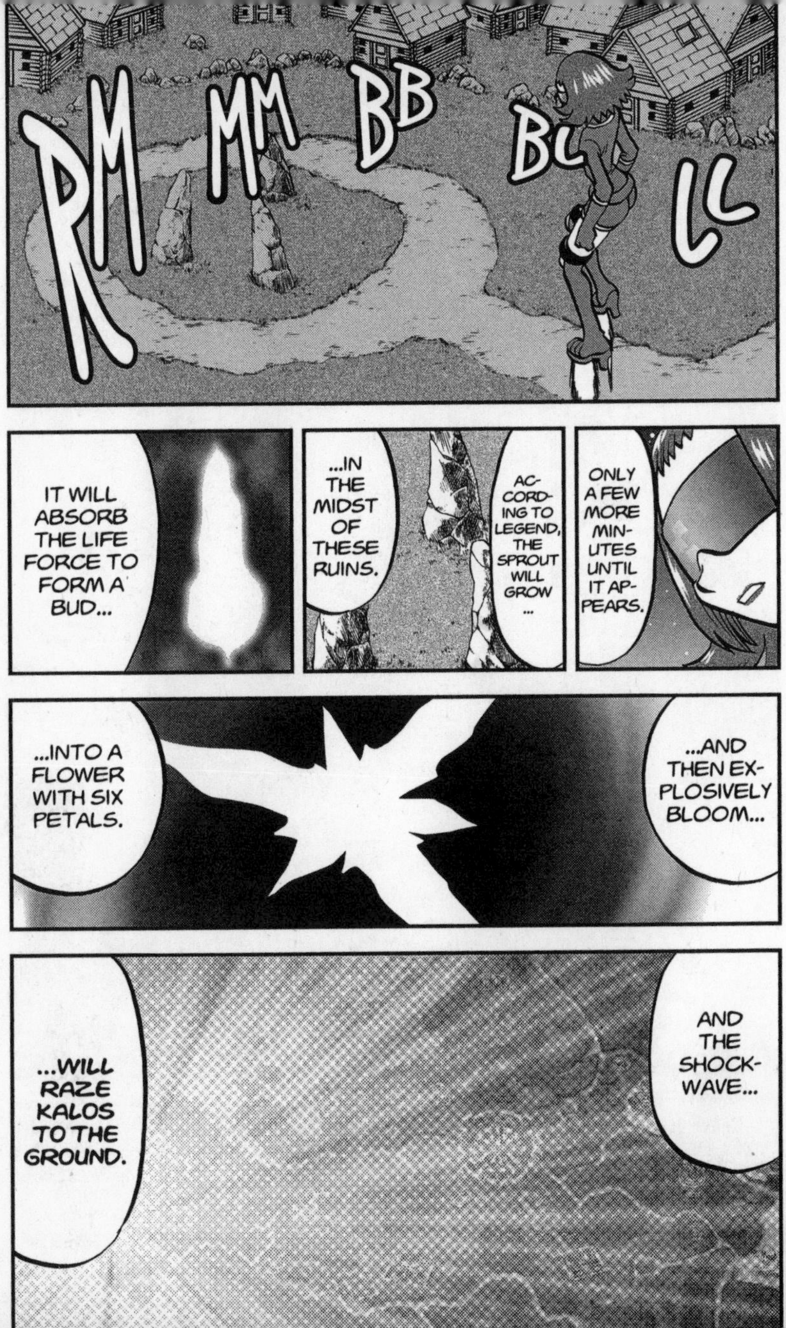
RM MM BB BL LL
ONLY A FEW MORE MINUTES UNTIL IT APPEARS.
ACCORDING TO LEGEND, THE SPROUT WILL GROW...
...IN THE MIDST OF THESE RUINS.
IT WILL ABSORB THE LIFE FORCE TO FORM A BUD...
...AND THEN EXPLOSIVELY BLOOM...
...INTO A FLOWER WITH SIX PETALS.
AND THE SHOCKWAVE...
...WILL RAZE KALOS TO THE GROUND.

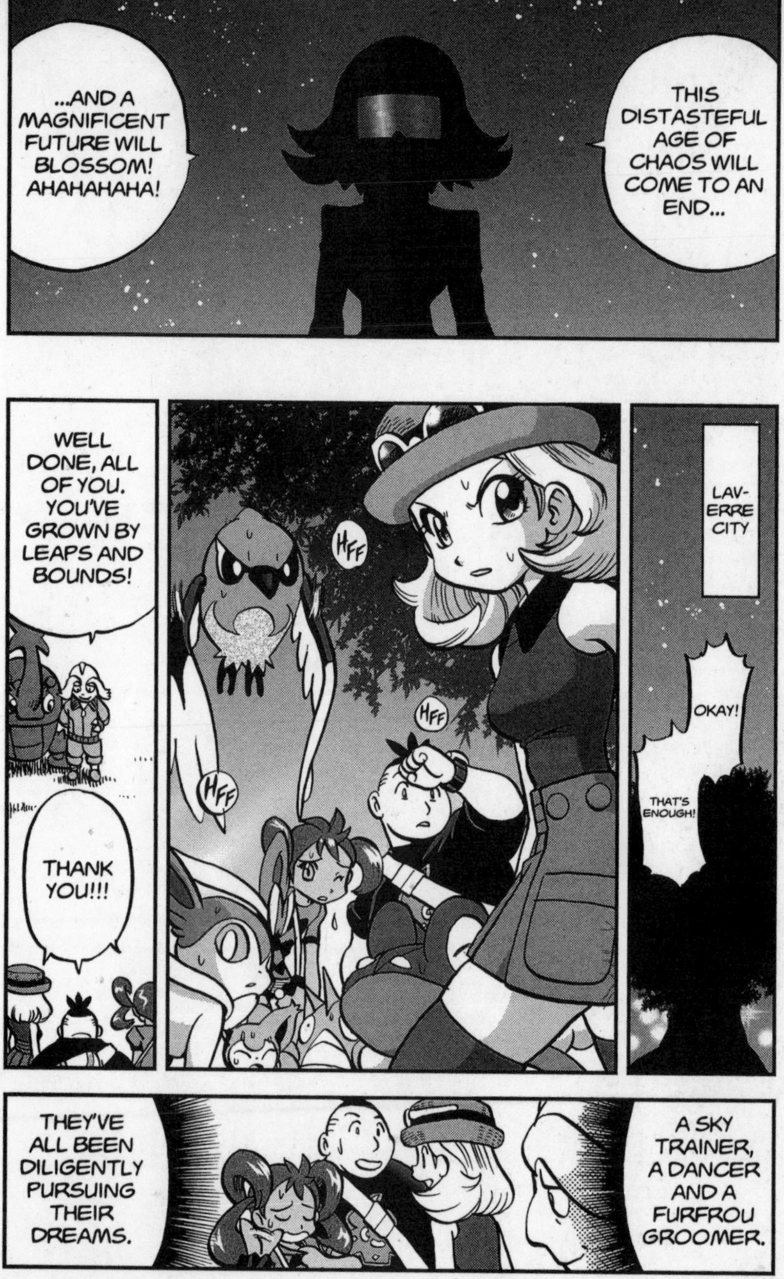
THIS DISTASTEFUL AGE OF CHAOS WILL COME TO AN END...
...AND A MAGNIFICENT FUTURE WILL BLOSSOM! AHAHAHAHA!
LAVERRE CITY
OKAY!
THAT'S ENOUGH!
HFF
HFF
HFF
WELL DONE, ALL OF YOU. YOU'VE GROWN BY LEAPS AND BOUNDS!
THANK YOU!!!
A SKY TRAINER, A DANCER AND A FURFROU GROOMER.
THEY'VE ALL BEEN DILIGENTLY PURSUING THEIR DREAMS.

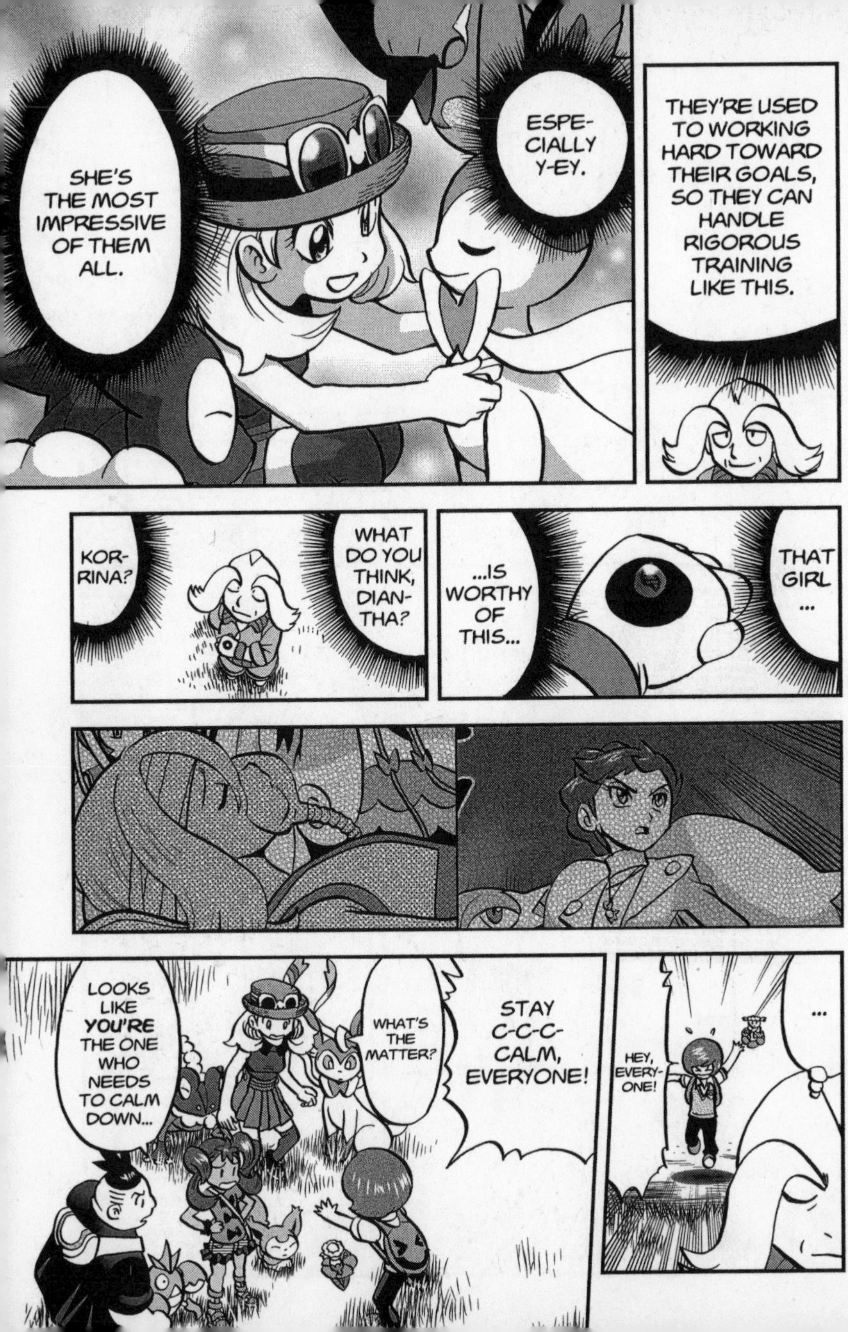
THEY'RE USED TO WORKING HARD TOWARD THEIR GOALS, SO THEY CAN HANDLE RIGOROUS TRAINING LIKE THIS.
ESPECIALLY Y-EY.
SHE'S THE MOST IMPRESSIVE OF THEM ALL.
THAT GIRL ...
...IS WORTHY OF THIS...
WHAT DO YOU THINK, DIANTHA?
KORRINA?
...
HEY, EVERYONE!
STAY C-C-C-CALM, EVERYONE!
WHAT'S THE MATTER?
LOOKS LIKE **YOU'RE** THE ONE WHO NEEDS TO CALM DOWN...

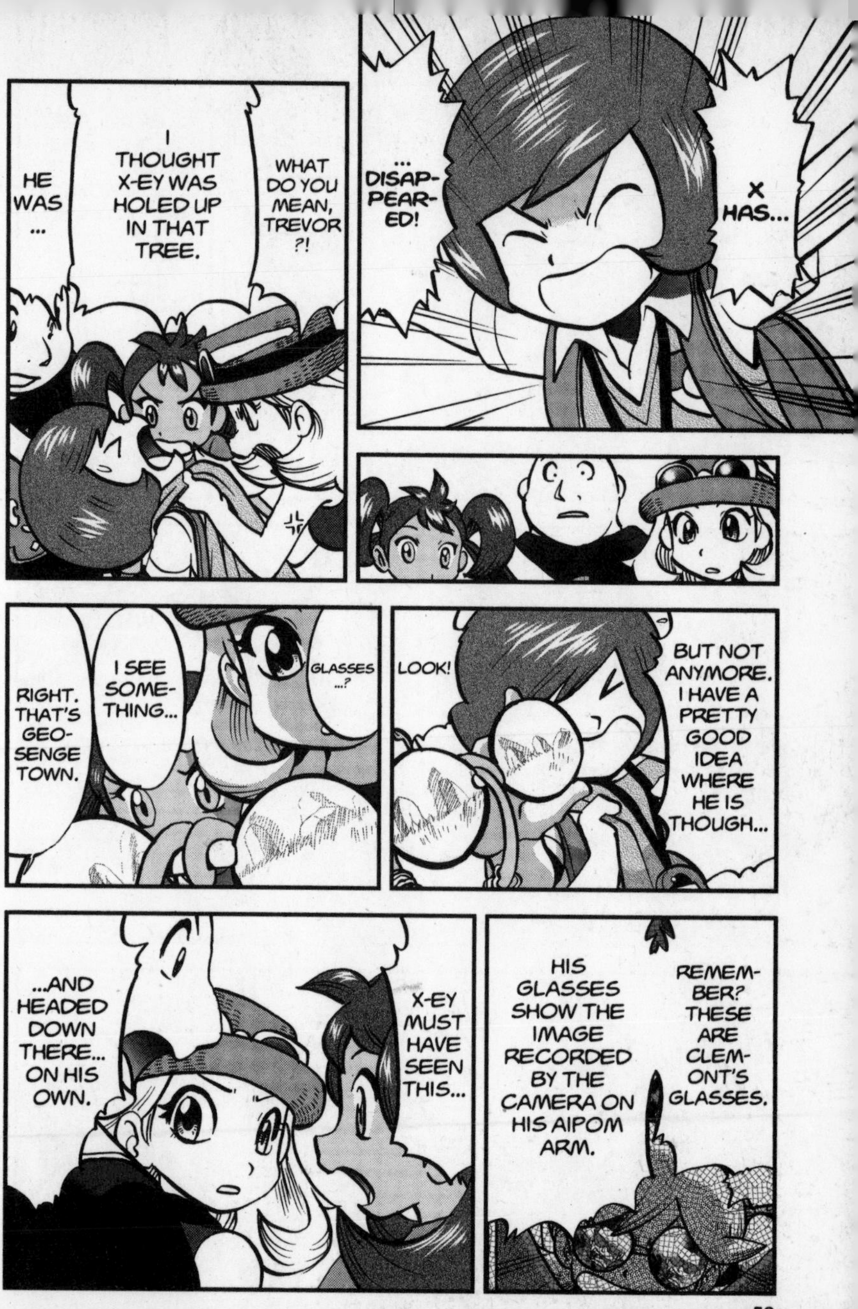
X HAS...
...DISAP-PEARED!
WHAT DO YOU MEAN, TREVOR?!
I THOUGHT X-EY WAS HOLED UP IN THAT TREE.
HE WAS...
BUT NOT ANYMORE. I HAVE A PRETTY GOOD IDEA WHERE HE IS THOUGH...
LOOK!
GLASSES...?
I SEE SOME-THING...
RIGHT. THAT'S GEO-SENGE TOWN.
REMEM-BER? THESE ARE CLEM-ONT'S GLASSES.
HIS GLASSES SHOW THE IMAGE RECORDED BY THE CAMERA ON HIS AIPOM ARM.
X-EY MUST HAVE SEEN THIS...
...AND HEADED DOWN THERE... ON HIS OWN.

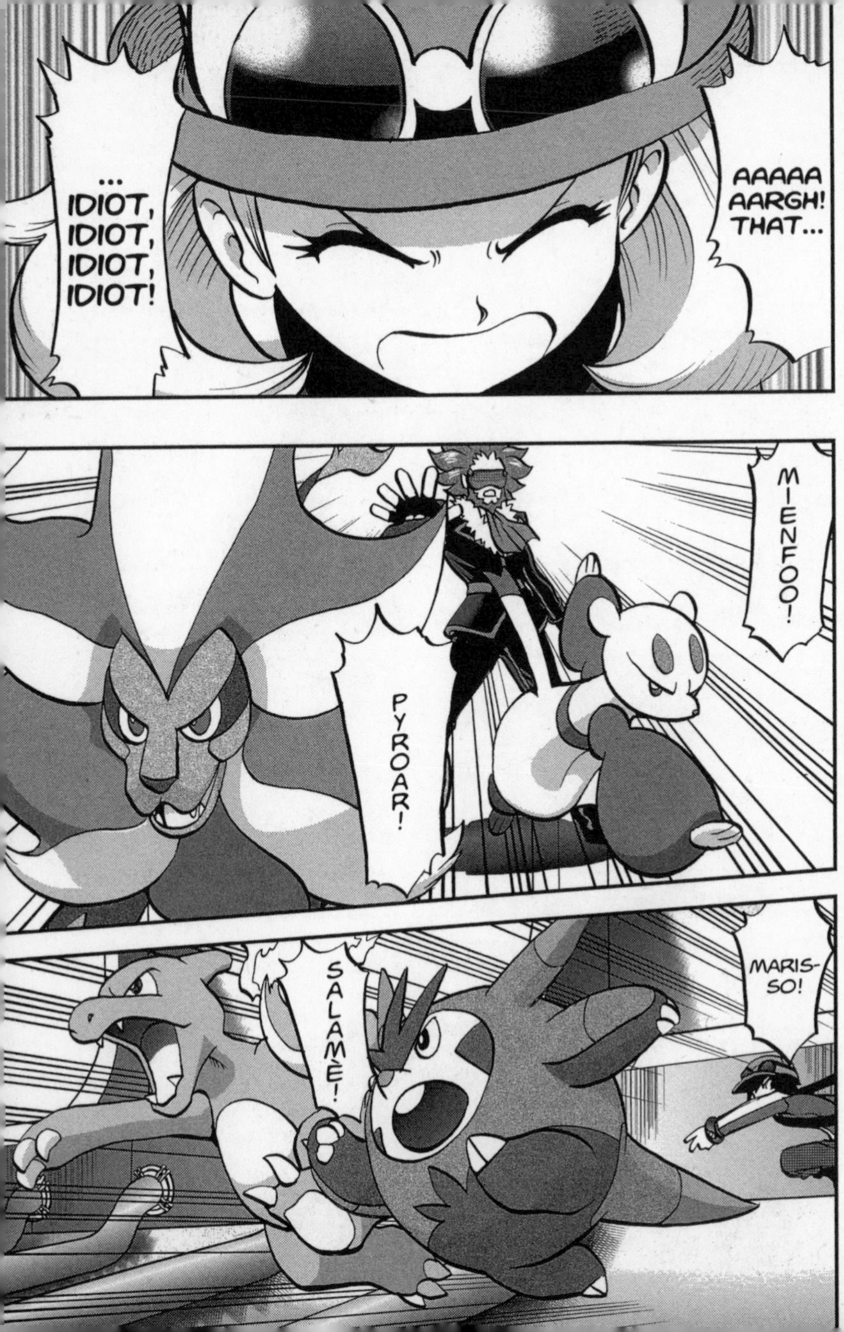
AAAAA AARGH! THAT...
...IDIOT, IDIOT, IDIOT, IDIOT!
MIENFOO!
PYROAR!
MARIS-SO!
SALAMÈ!

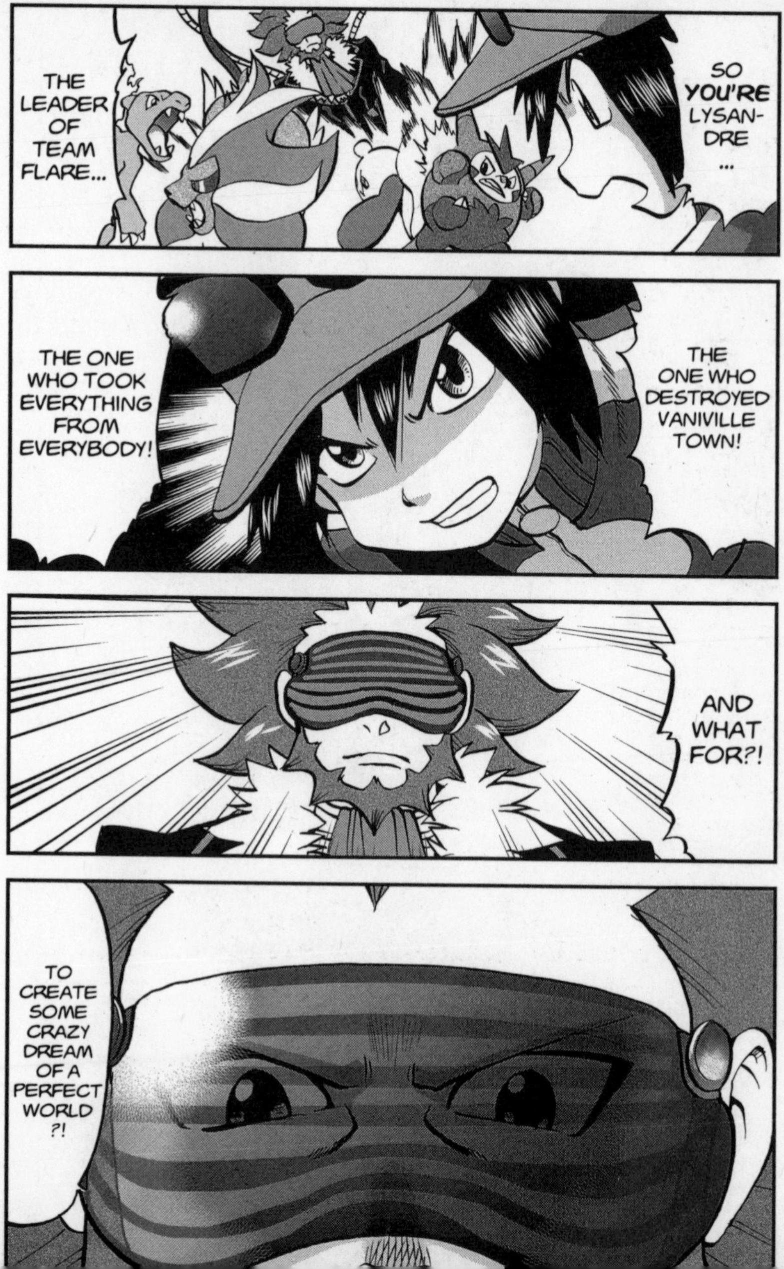
SO YOU'RE LYSANDRE...
THE LEADER OF TEAM FLARE...
THE ONE WHO DESTROYED VANIVILLE TOWN!
THE ONE WHO TOOK EVERYTHING FROM EVERYBODY!
AND WHAT FOR?!
TO CREATE SOME CRAZY DREAM OF A PERFECT WORLD?!

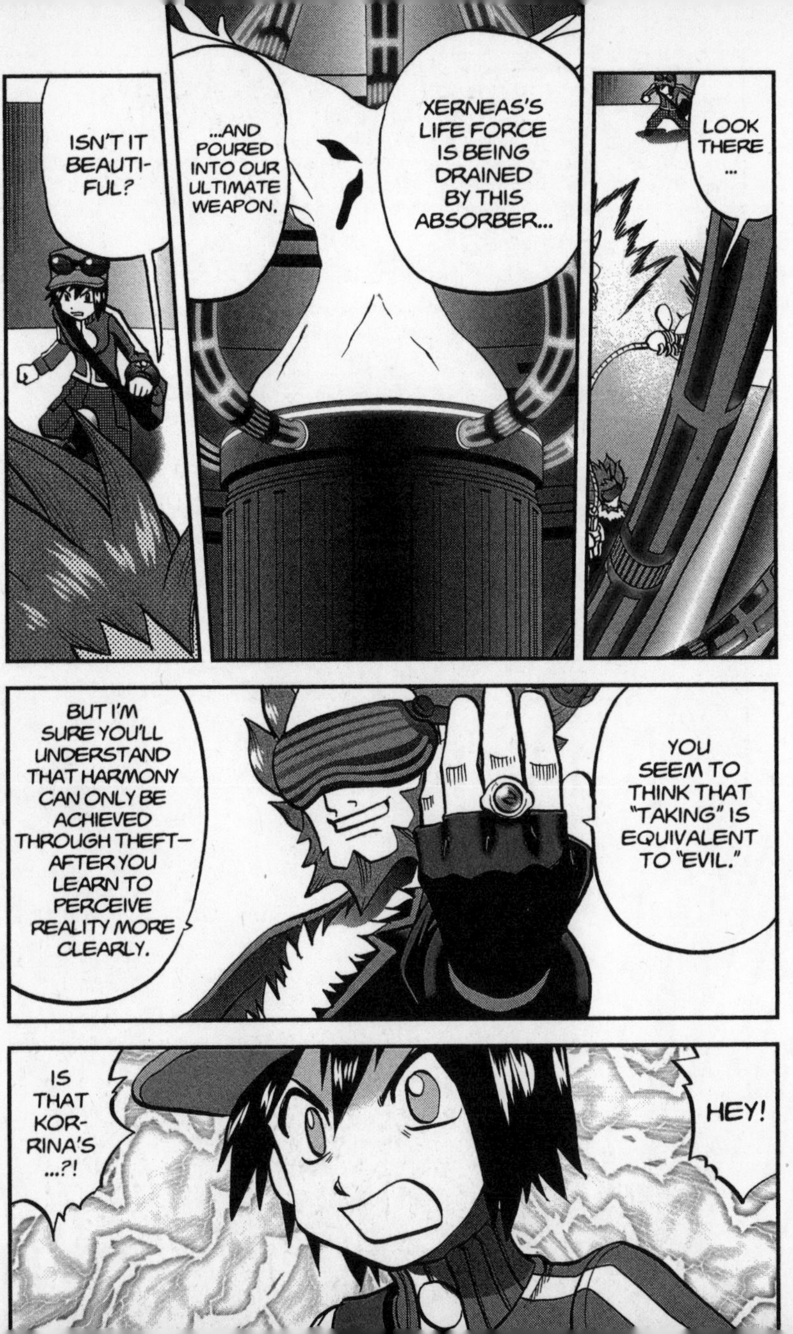
LOOK THERE ...
XERNEAS'S LIFE FORCE IS BEING DRAINED BY THIS ABSORBER...
...AND POURED INTO OUR ULTIMATE WEAPON.
ISN'T IT BEAUTI-FUL?
YOU SEEM TO THINK THAT "TAKING" IS EQUIVALENT TO "EVIL."
BUT I'M SURE YOU'LL UNDERSTAND THAT HARMONY CAN ONLY BE ACHIEVED THROUGH THEFT— AFTER YOU LEARN TO PERCEIVE REALITY MORE CLEARLY.
HEY!
IS THAT KOR-RINA'S ...?!

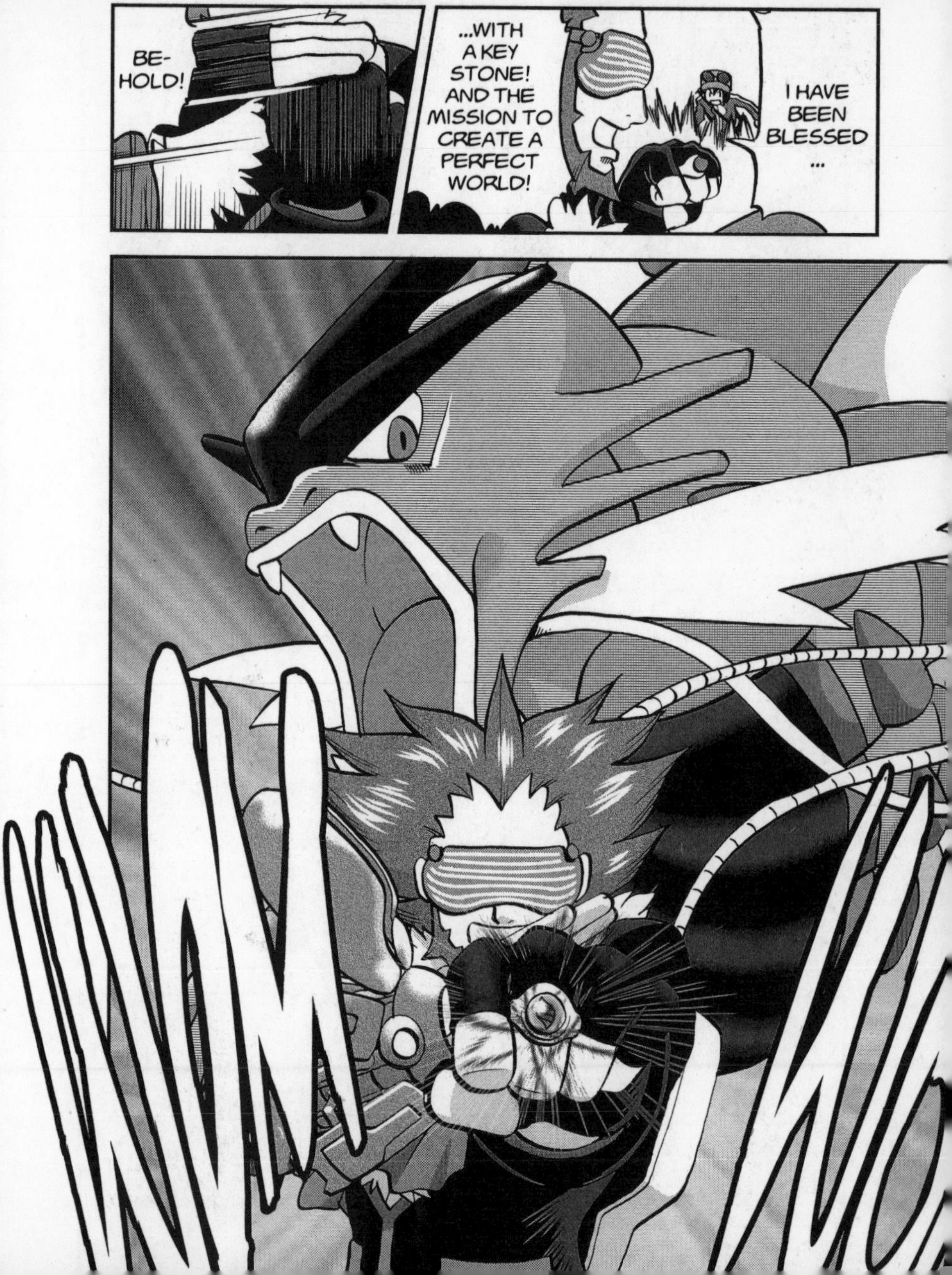
I HAVE BEEN BLESSED ...
...WITH A KEY STONE! AND THE MISSION TO CREATE A PERFECT WORLD!
BE-HOLD!

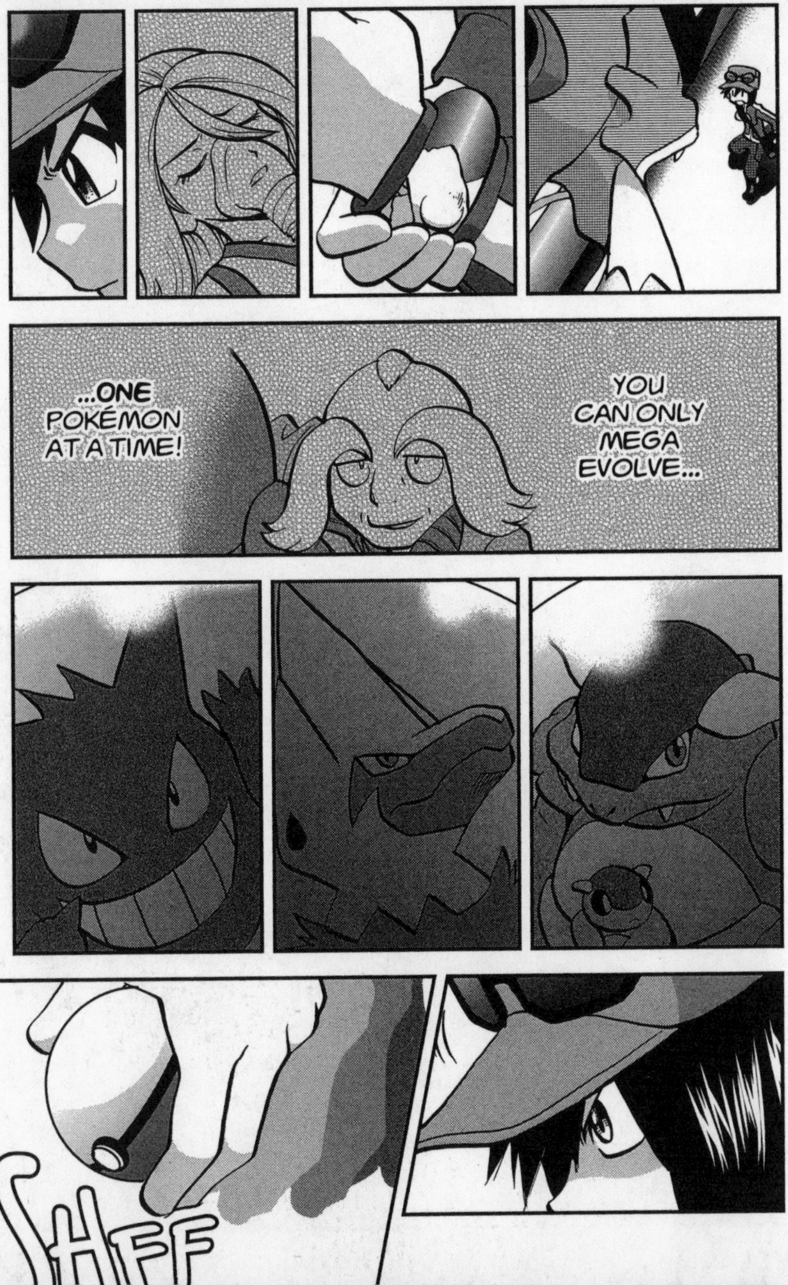
YOU CAN ONLY MEGA EVOLVE...
...ONE POKÉMON AT A TIME!
SHFF

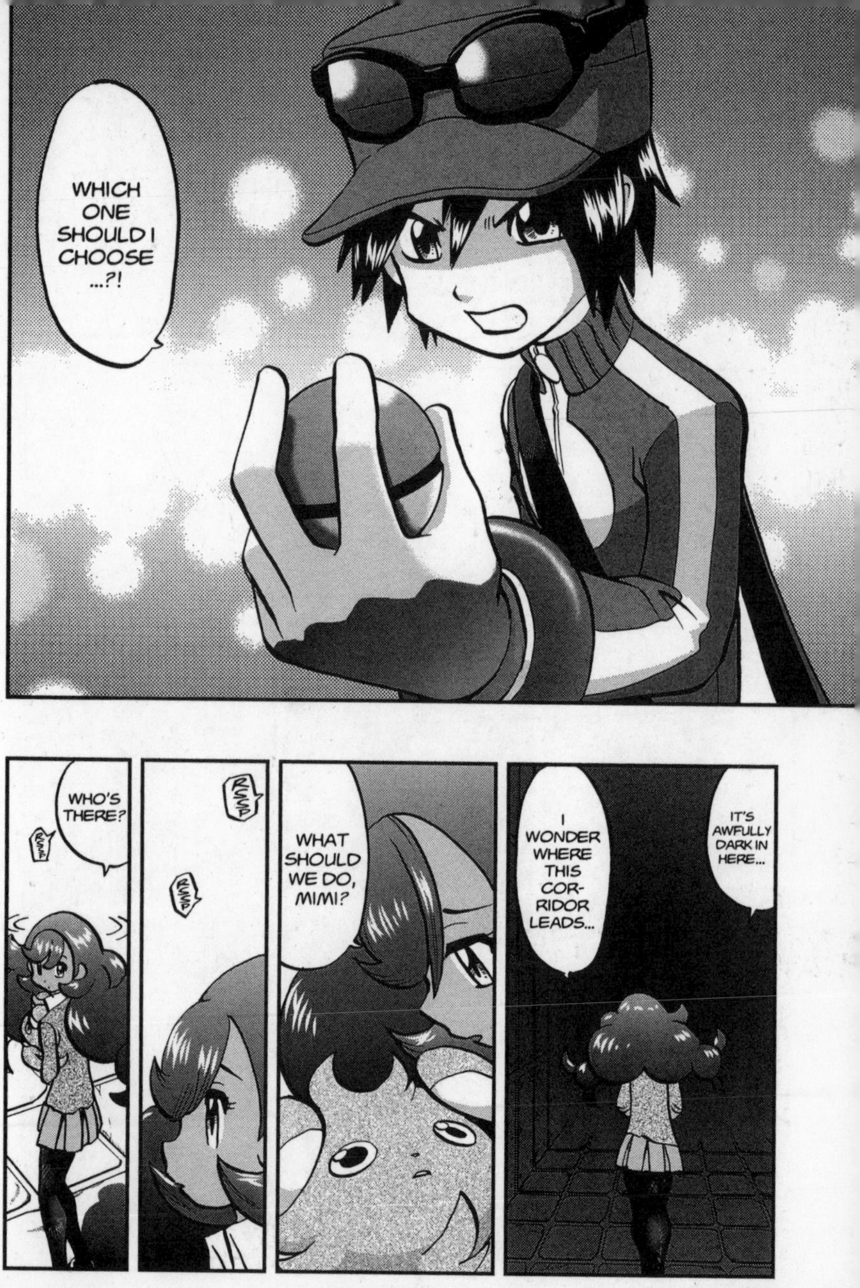
WHICH ONE SHOULD I CHOOSE ...?!
IT'S AWFULLY DARK IN HERE...
I WONDER WHERE THIS COR-RIDOR LEADS...
WHAT SHOULD WE DO, MIMI?
RUMP
RUMP
WHO'S THERE?
RUMP

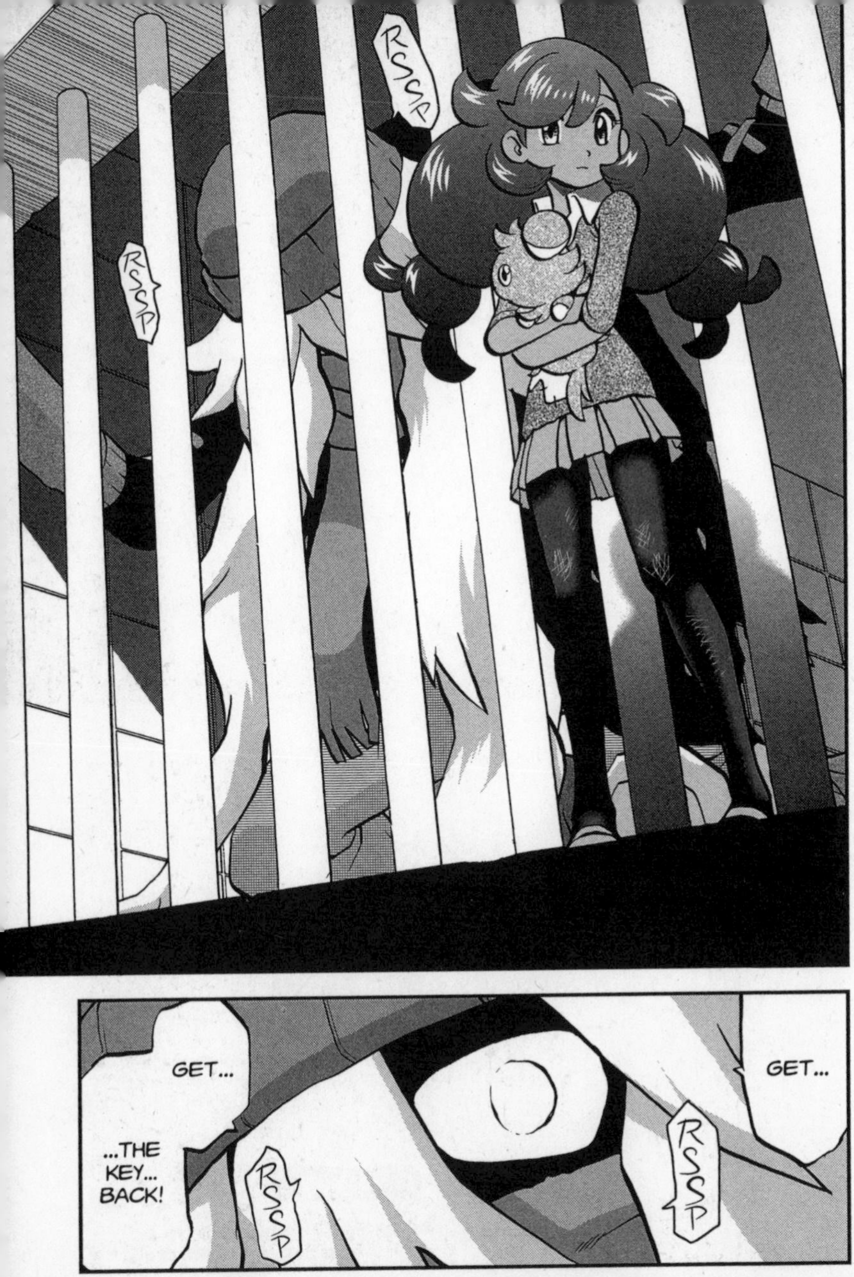
RSSP
RSSP
GET...
RSSP
GET...
...THE KEY... BACK!
RSSP

Current Location

Route 11
Miroir Way

One can feel the power of the earth's
interior from the crystals that sprout
along this mountain path.

▼

A town lined with mysterious stones
and encircled by strange ruins of old.

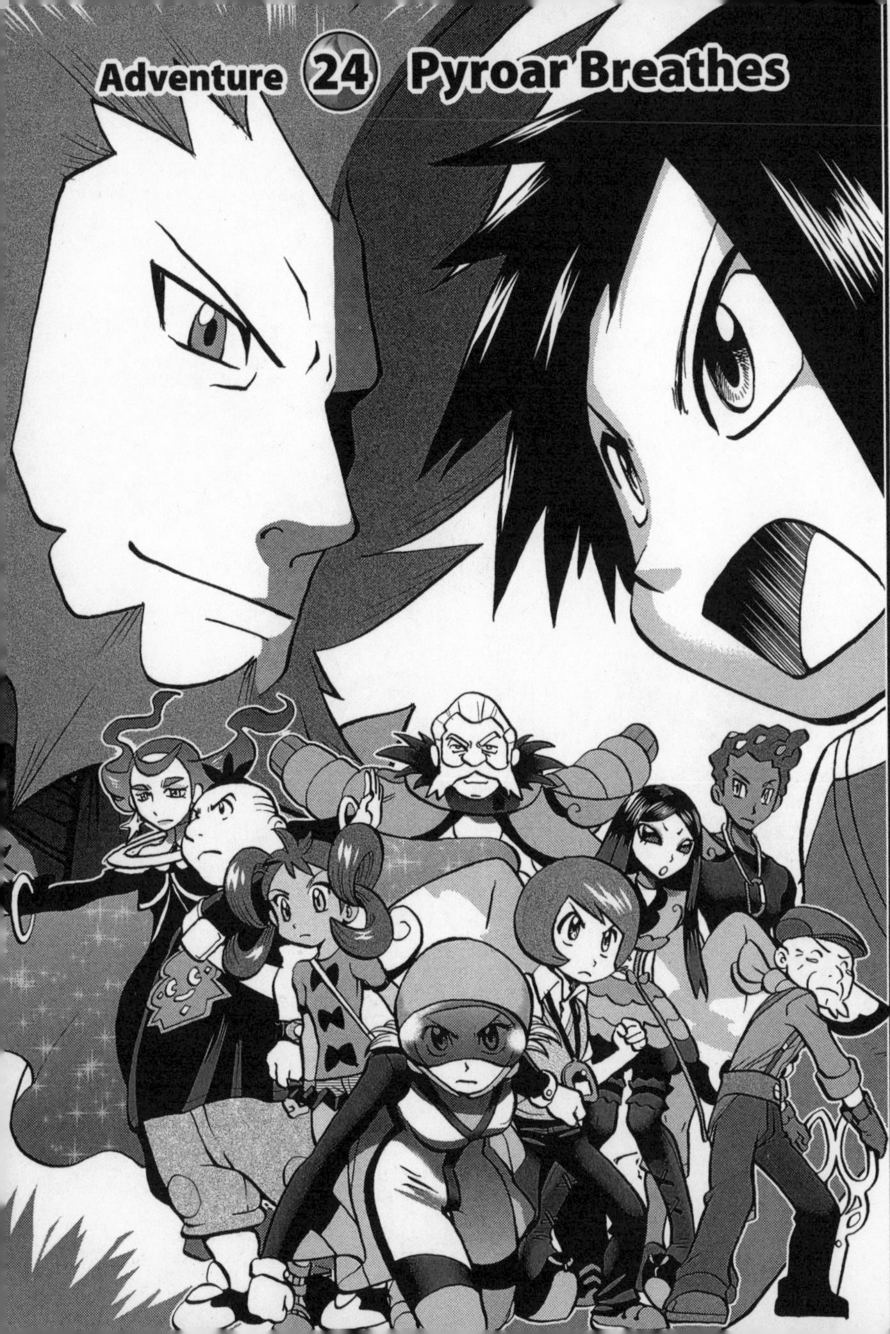
Adventure 24 Pyroar Breathes

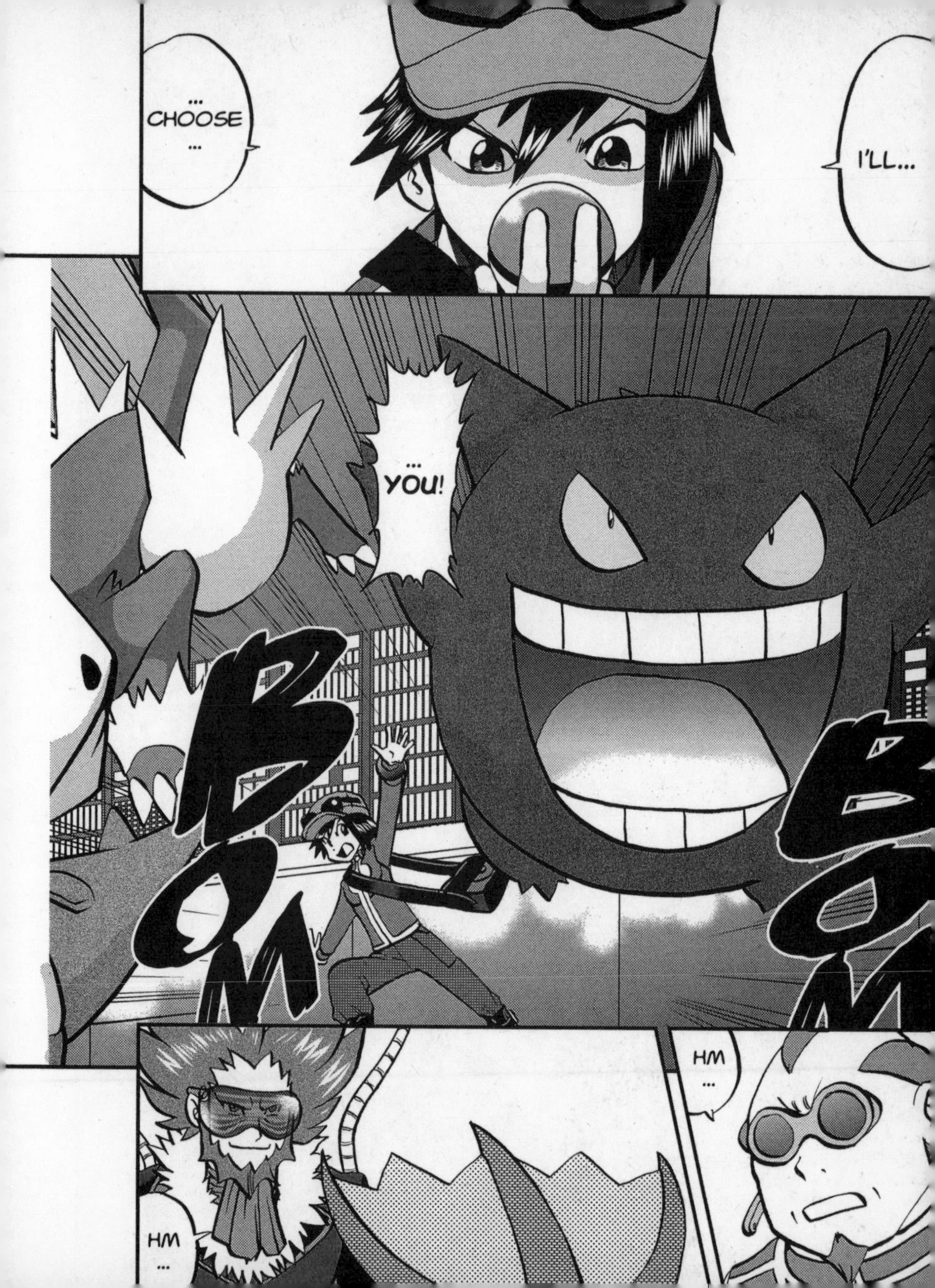
I'LL...
...CHOOSE...
...YOU!
BOM
BOM
HM...
HM...

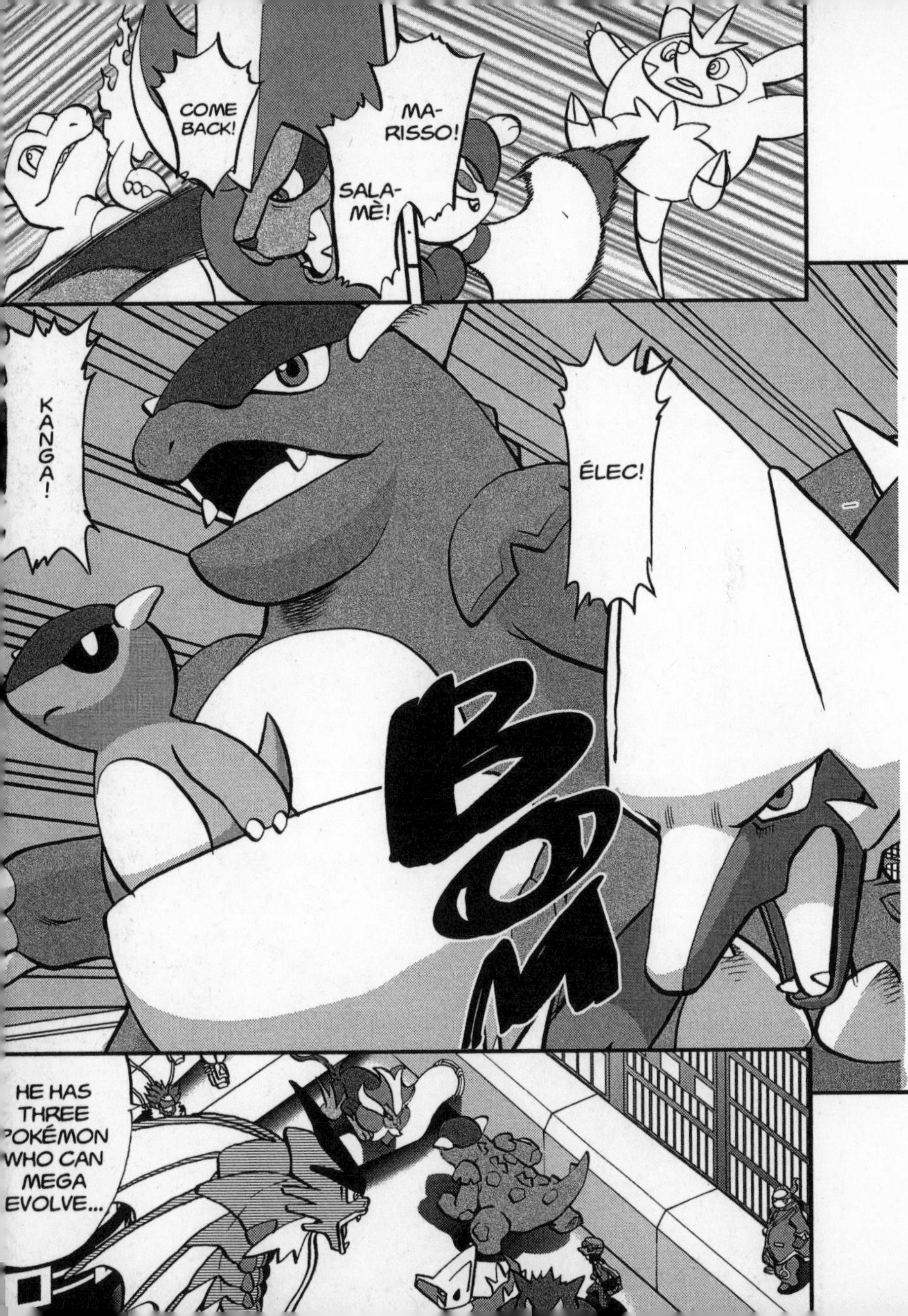
MA-RISSO!
COME BACK!
SALA-MÈ!
ÉLEC!
KANGA!
BOOM
HE HAS THREE POKÉMON WHO CAN MEGA EVOLVE...

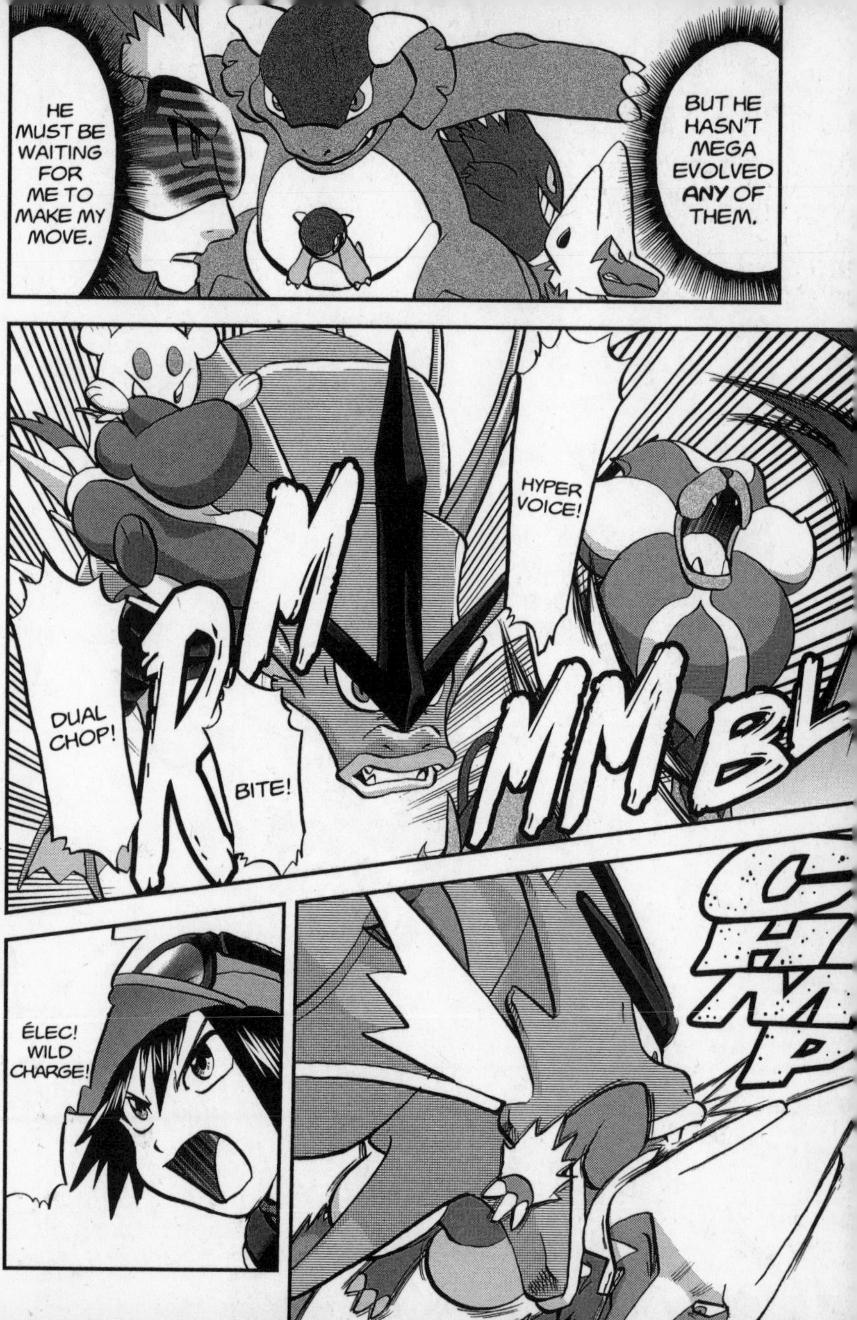
BUT HE HASN'T MEGA EVOLVED ANY OF THEM.
HE MUST BE WAITING FOR ME TO MAKE MY MOVE.
HYPER VOICE!
RM
MMBL
BITE!
DUAL CHOP!
CHMP
ÉLEC! WILD CHARGE!

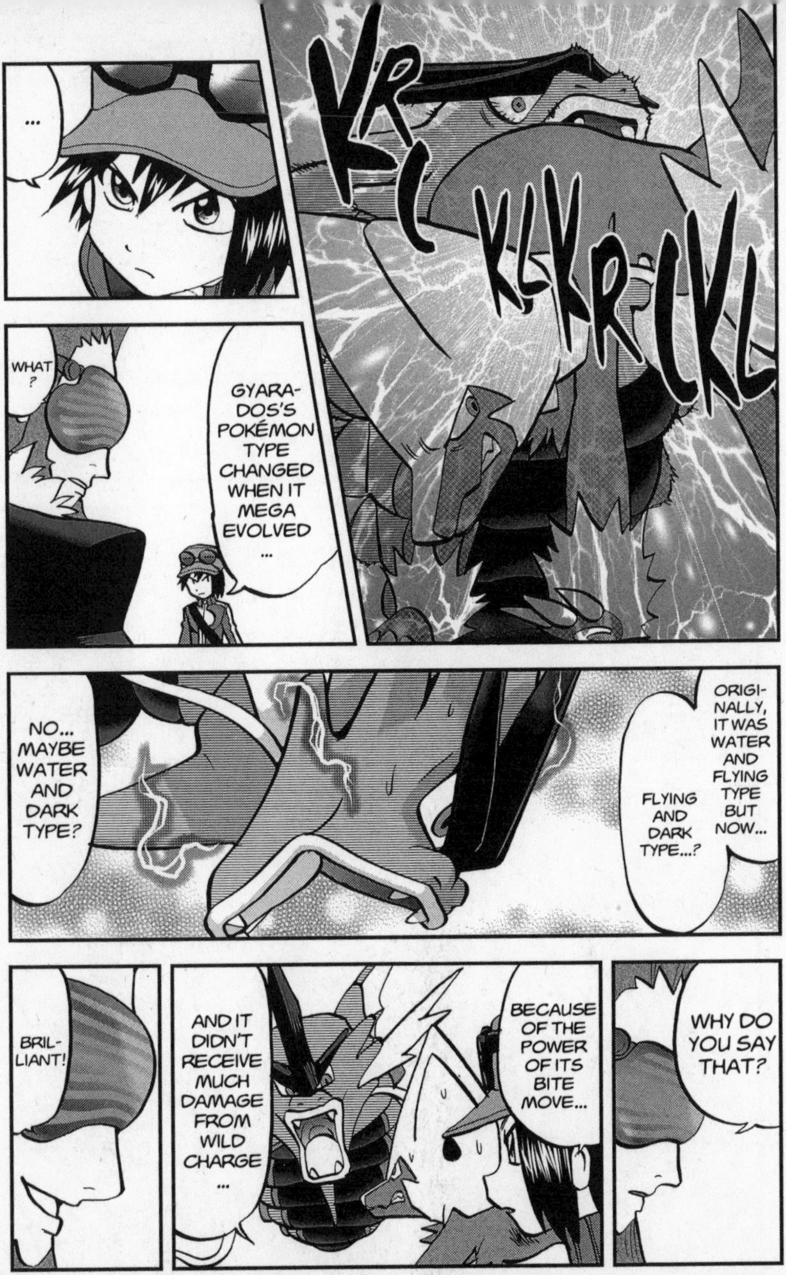
KRI KLKRICKL
...
GYARADOS'S POKÉMON TYPE CHANGED WHEN IT MEGA EVOLVED ...
WHAT?
ORIGINALLY, IT WAS WATER AND FLYING TYPE BUT NOW...
FLYING AND DARK TYPE...?
NO... MAYBE WATER AND DARK TYPE?
WHY DO YOU SAY THAT?
BECAUSE OF THE POWER OF ITS BITE MOVE...
AND IT DIDN'T RECEIVE MUCH DAMAGE FROM WILD CHARGE ...
BRILLIANT!

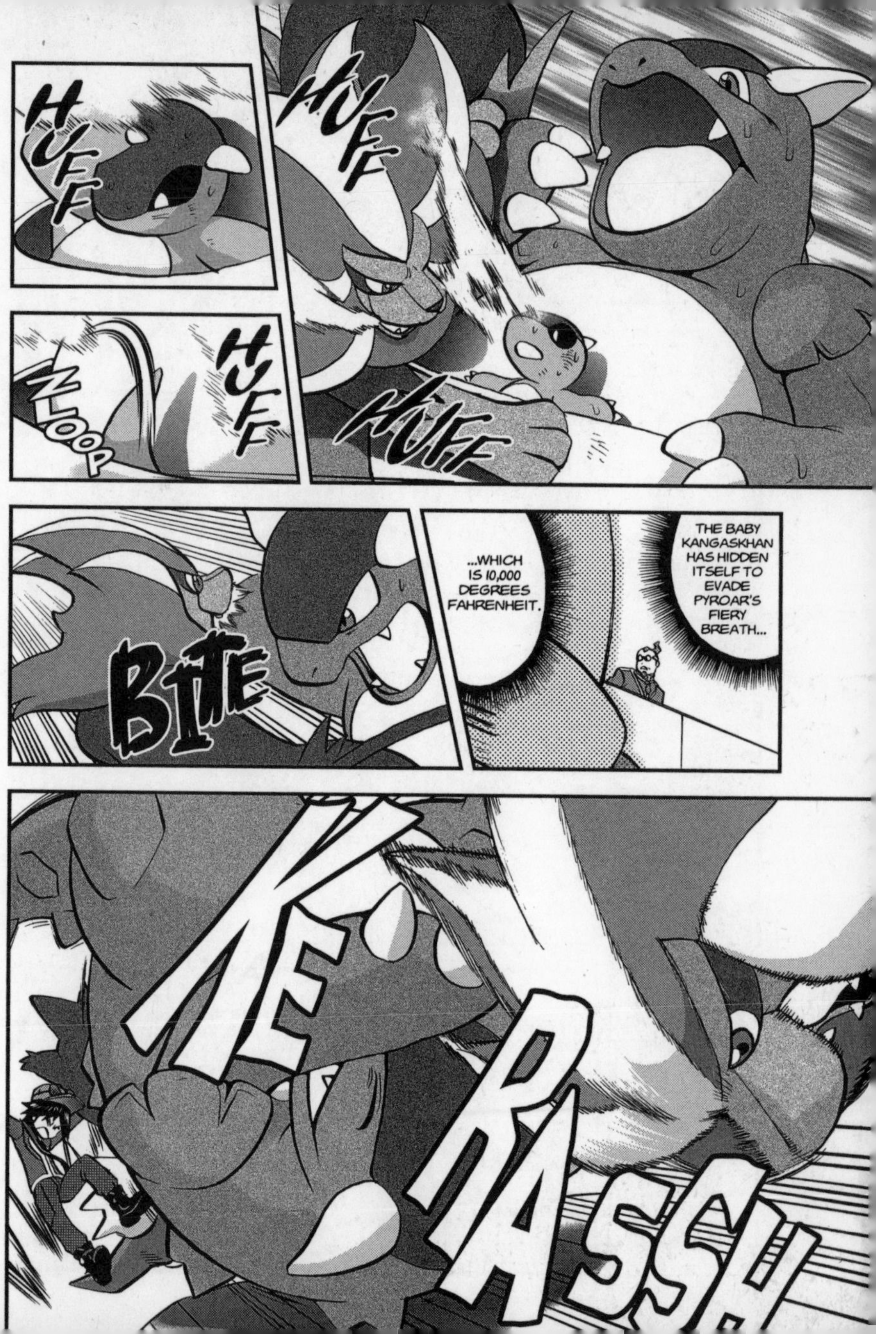
HUFF
HUFF
HUFF
SLOOP
HUFF
THE BABY KANGASKHAN HAS HIDDEN ITSELF TO EVADE PYROAR'S FIERY BREATH...
...WHICH IS 10,000 DEGREES FAHRENHEIT.
BITE
KERASSH

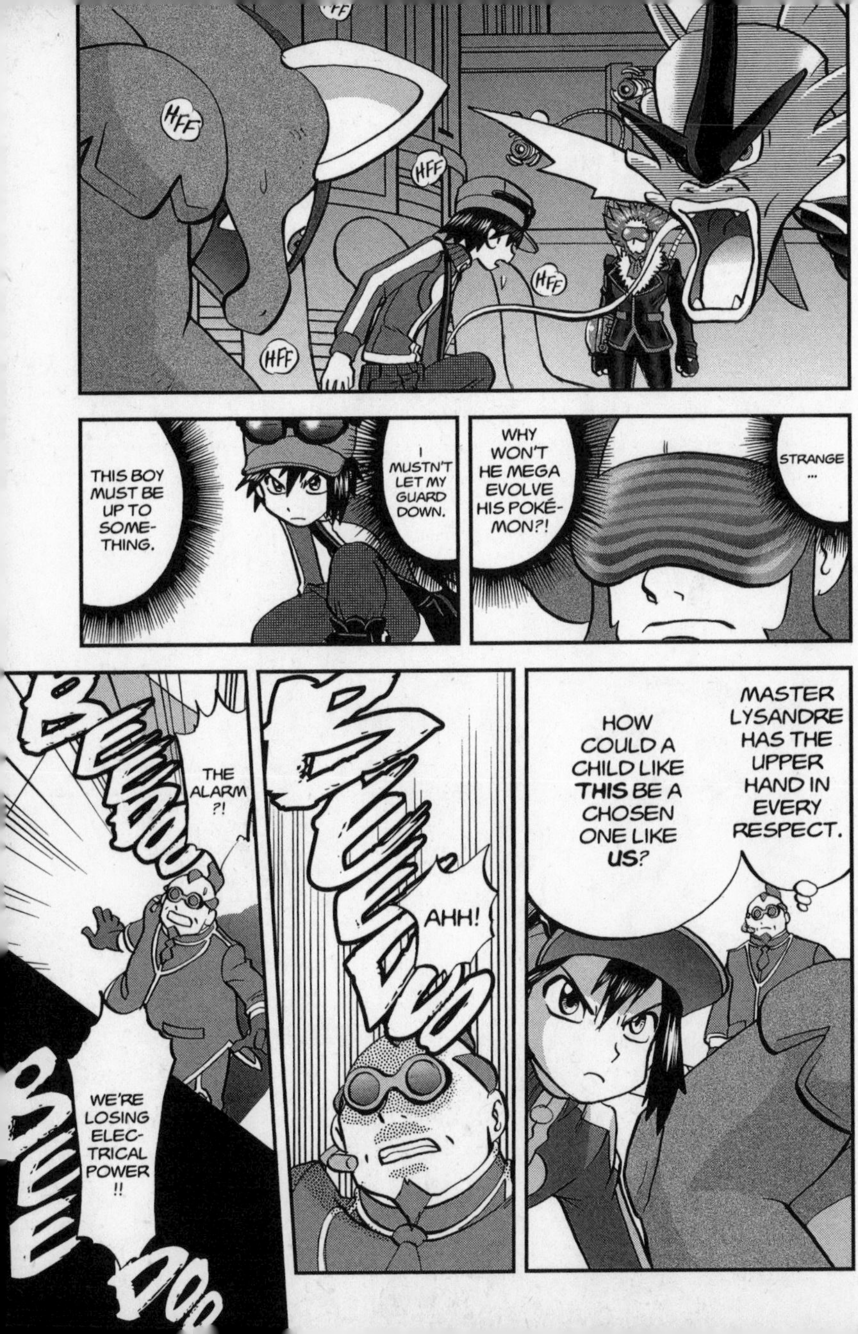
HFF
HFF
HFF
HFF
STRANGE ...
WHY WON'T HE MEGA EVOLVE HIS POKÉMON?!
I MUSTN'T LET MY GUARD DOWN.
THIS BOY MUST BE UP TO SOME-THING.
MASTER LYSANDRE HAS THE UPPER HAND IN EVERY RESPECT.
HOW COULD A CHILD LIKE **THIS** BE A CHOSEN ONE LIKE **US**?
AHH!
THE ALARM?!
WE'RE LOSING ELEC-TRICAL POWER!!

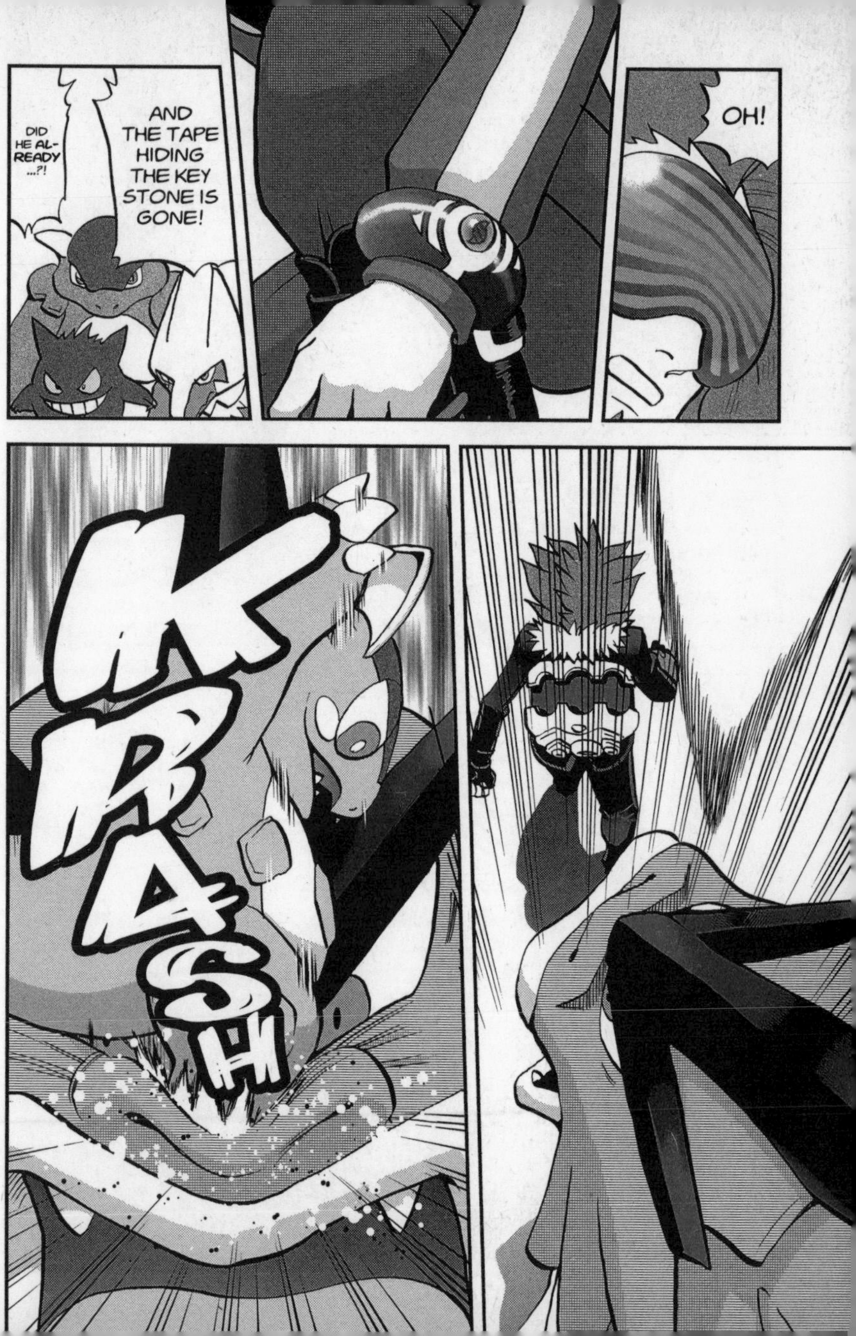
OH!
AND THE TAPE HIDING THE KEY STONE IS GONE!
DID HE AL-READY ...?!
KRASH

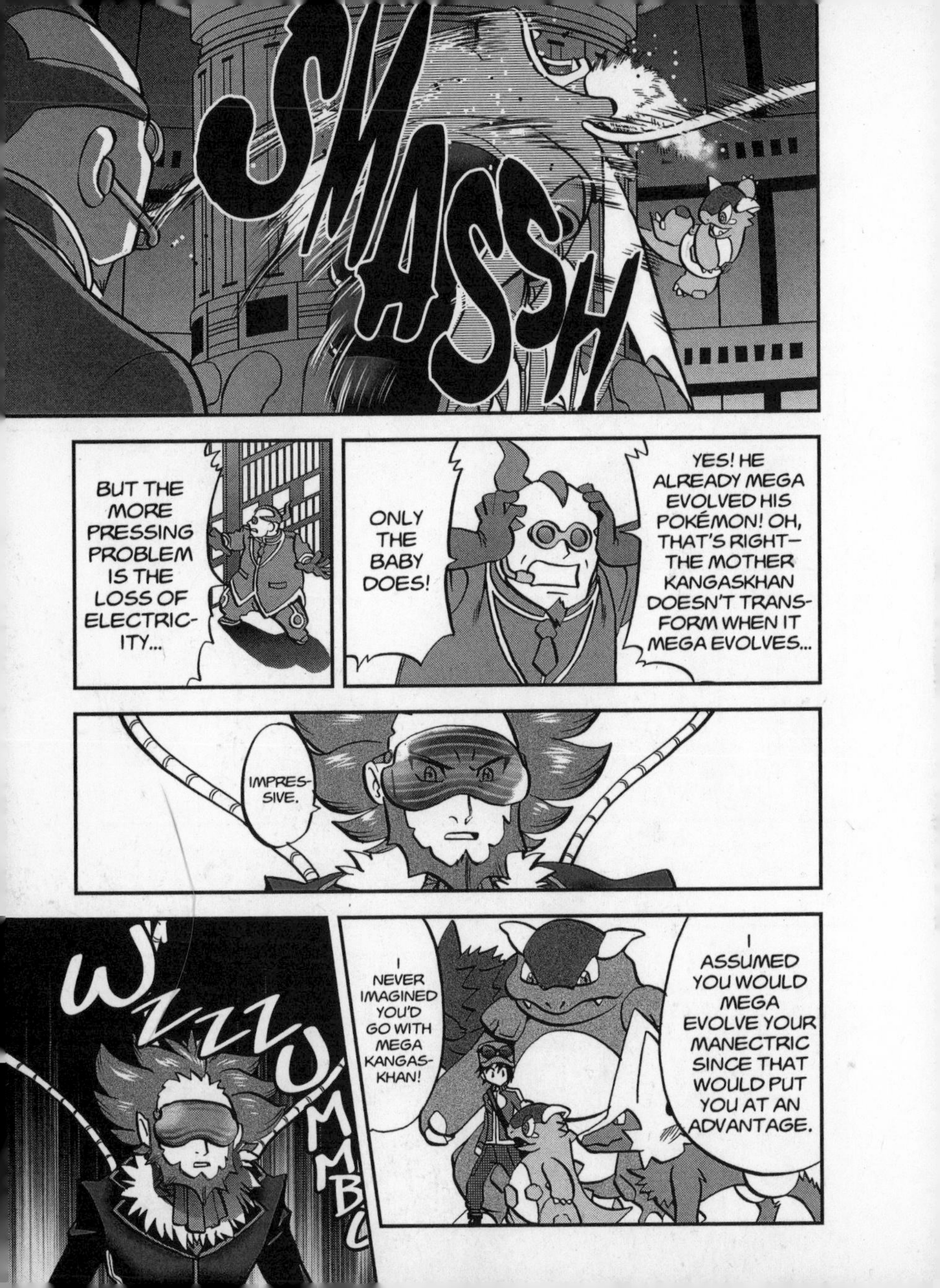
SMASH
YES! HE ALREADY MEGA EVOLVED HIS POKÉMON! OH, THAT'S RIGHT—THE MOTHER KANGASKHAN DOESN'T TRANSFORM WHEN IT MEGA EVOLVES...
ONLY THE BABY DOES!
BUT THE MORE PRESSING PROBLEM IS THE LOSS OF ELECTRICITY...
IMPRESSIVE.
I ASSUMED YOU WOULD MEGA EVOLVE YOUR MANECTRIC SINCE THAT WOULD PUT YOU AT AN ADVANTAGE.
I NEVER IMAGINED YOU'D GO WITH MEGA KANGASKHAN!
WZZZUMMB

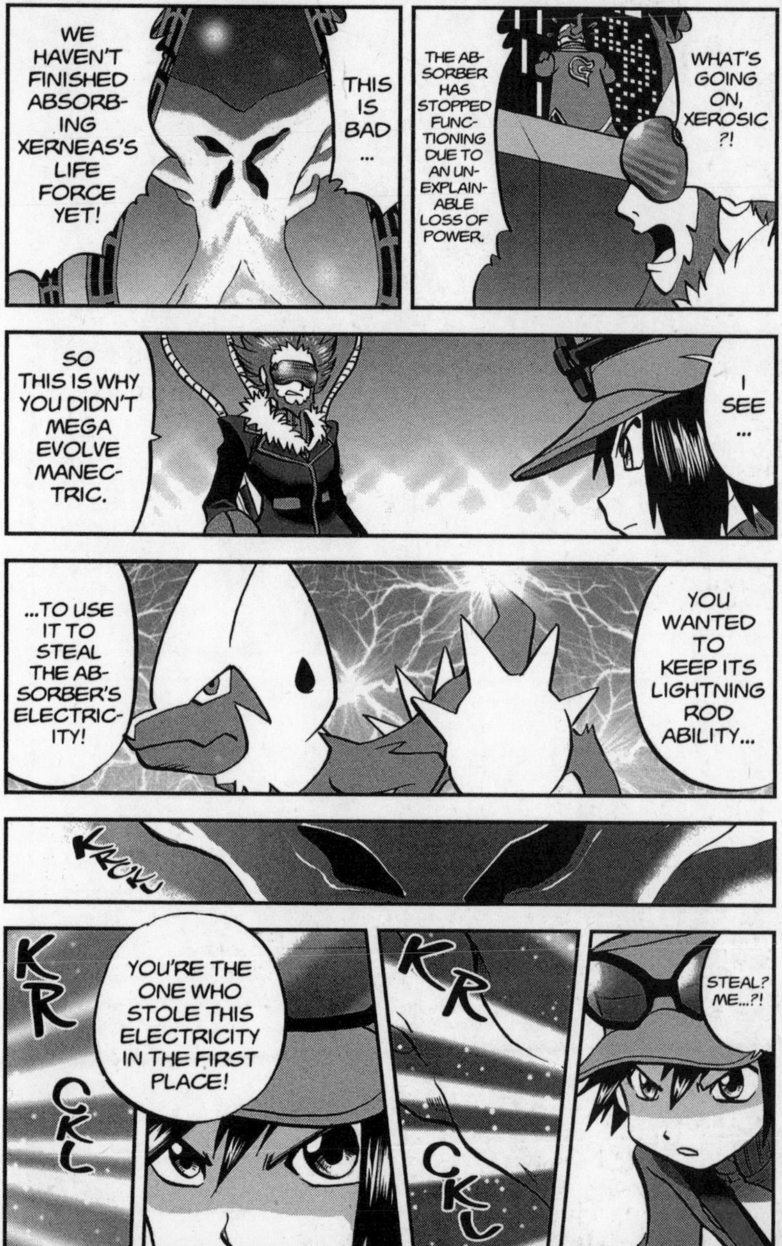
WHAT'S GOING ON, XEROSIC?!
THE ABSORBER HAS STOPPED FUNCTIONING DUE TO AN UNEXPLAINABLE LOSS OF POWER.
THIS IS BAD...
WE HAVEN'T FINISHED ABSORBING XERNEAS'S LIFE FORCE YET!
I SEE...
SO THIS IS WHY YOU DIDN'T MEGA EVOLVE MANECTRIC.
YOU WANTED TO KEEP ITS LIGHTNING ROD ABILITY...
...TO USE IT TO STEAL THE ABSORBER'S ELECTRICITY!
KRCKL
STEAL? ME...?!
KR
CKL
YOU'RE THE ONE WHO STOLE THIS ELECTRICITY IN THE FIRST PLACE!
KR
CKL

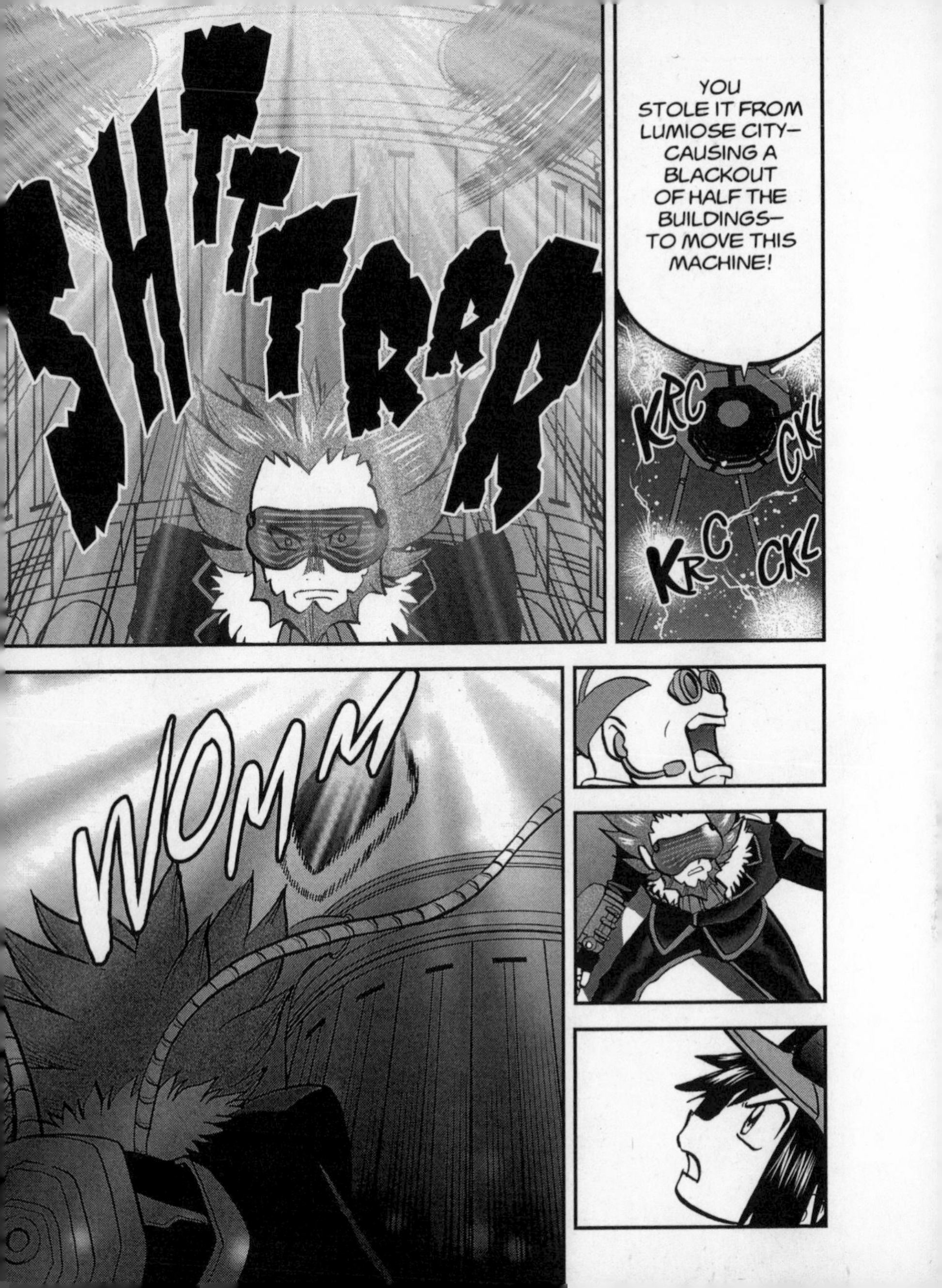
YOU STOLE IT FROM LUMIOSE CITY— CAUSING A BLACKOUT OF HALF THE BUILDINGS— TO MOVE THIS MACHINE!
KRC CKL
KRC CKL
SHTRRR
WOMM

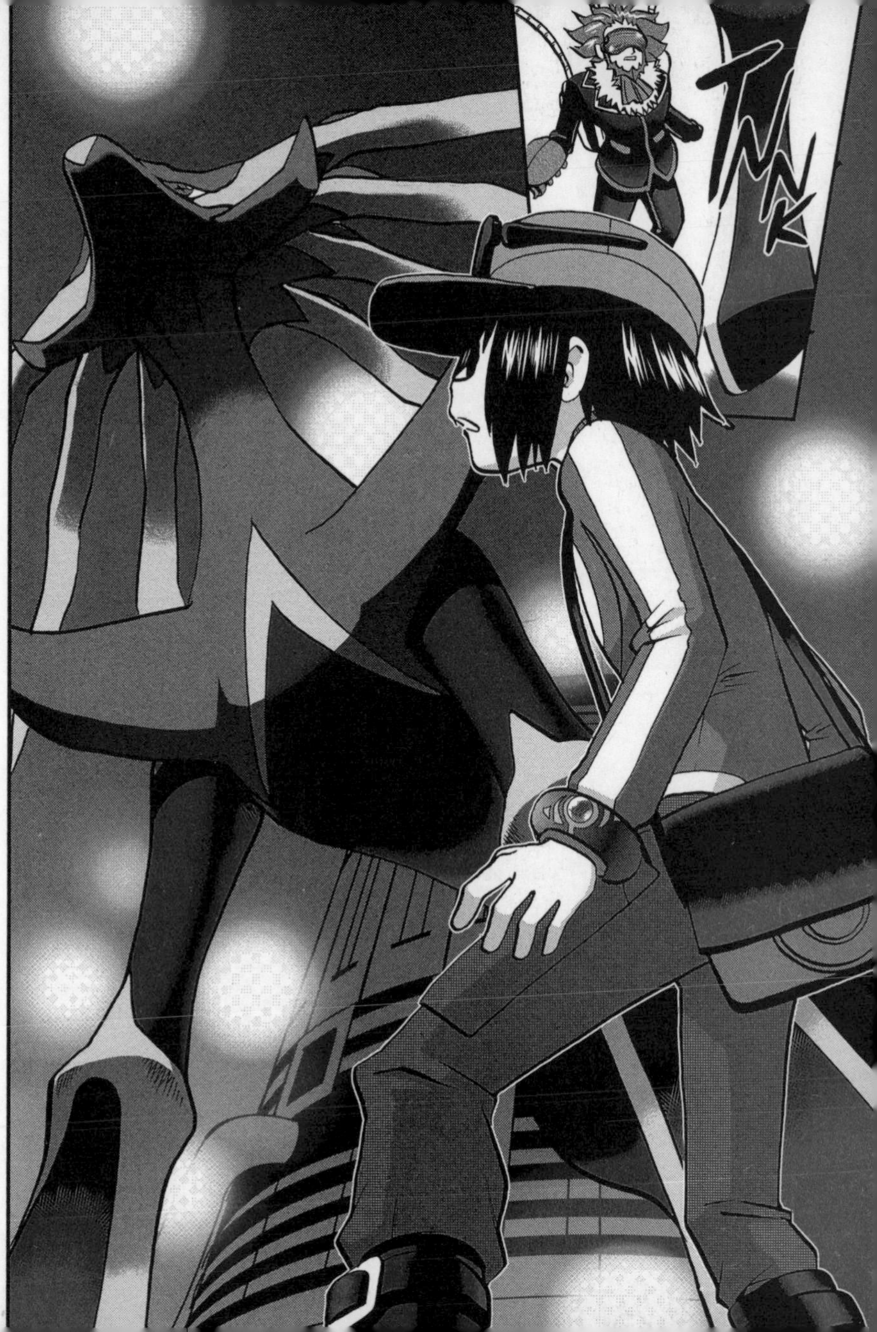
THNK

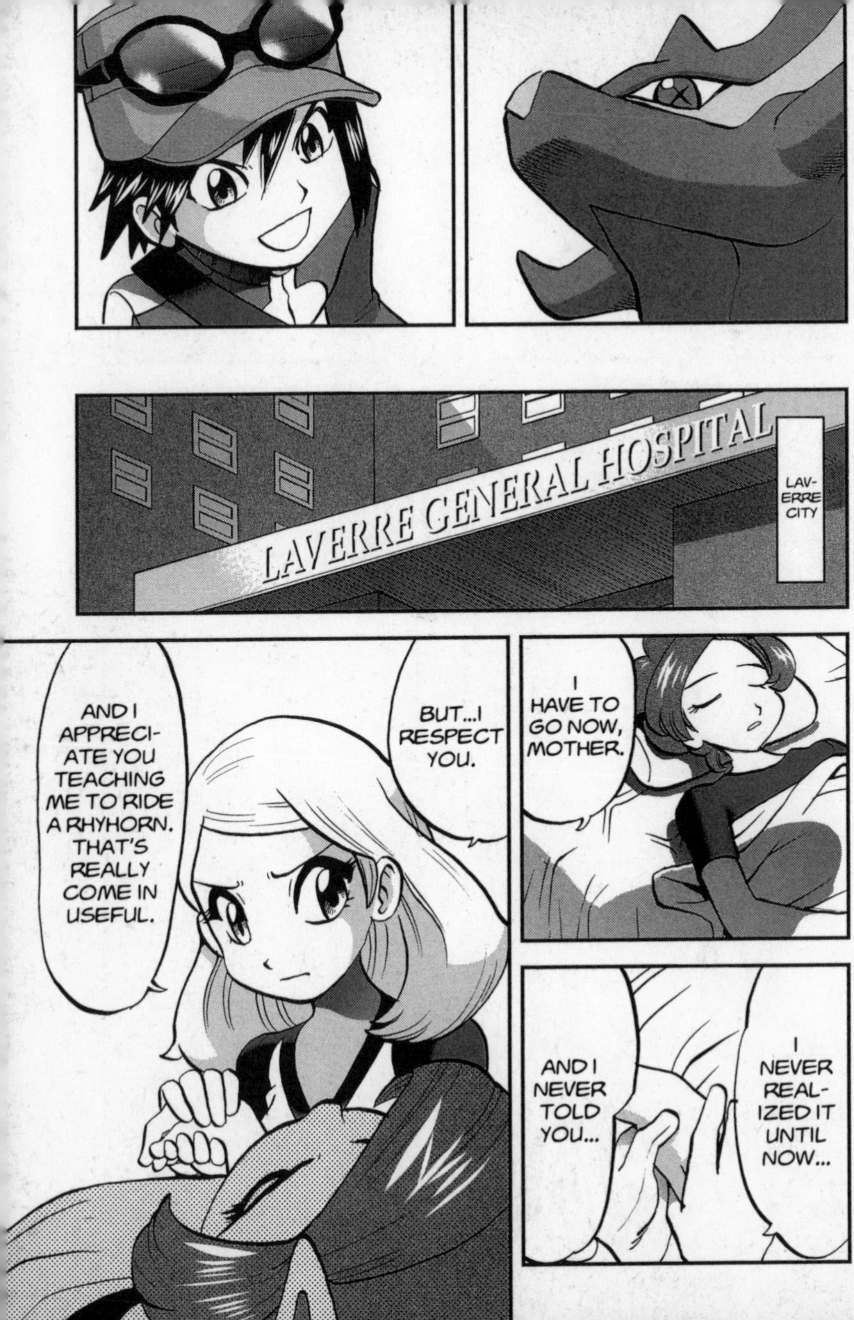
LAVERRE GENERAL HOSPITAL
LAVERRE CITY
I HAVE TO GO NOW, MOTHER.
I NEVER REALIZED IT UNTIL NOW...
AND I NEVER TOLD YOU...
BUT...I RESPECT YOU.
AND I APPRECIATE YOU TEACHING ME TO RIDE A RHYHORN. THAT'S REALLY COME IN USEFUL.

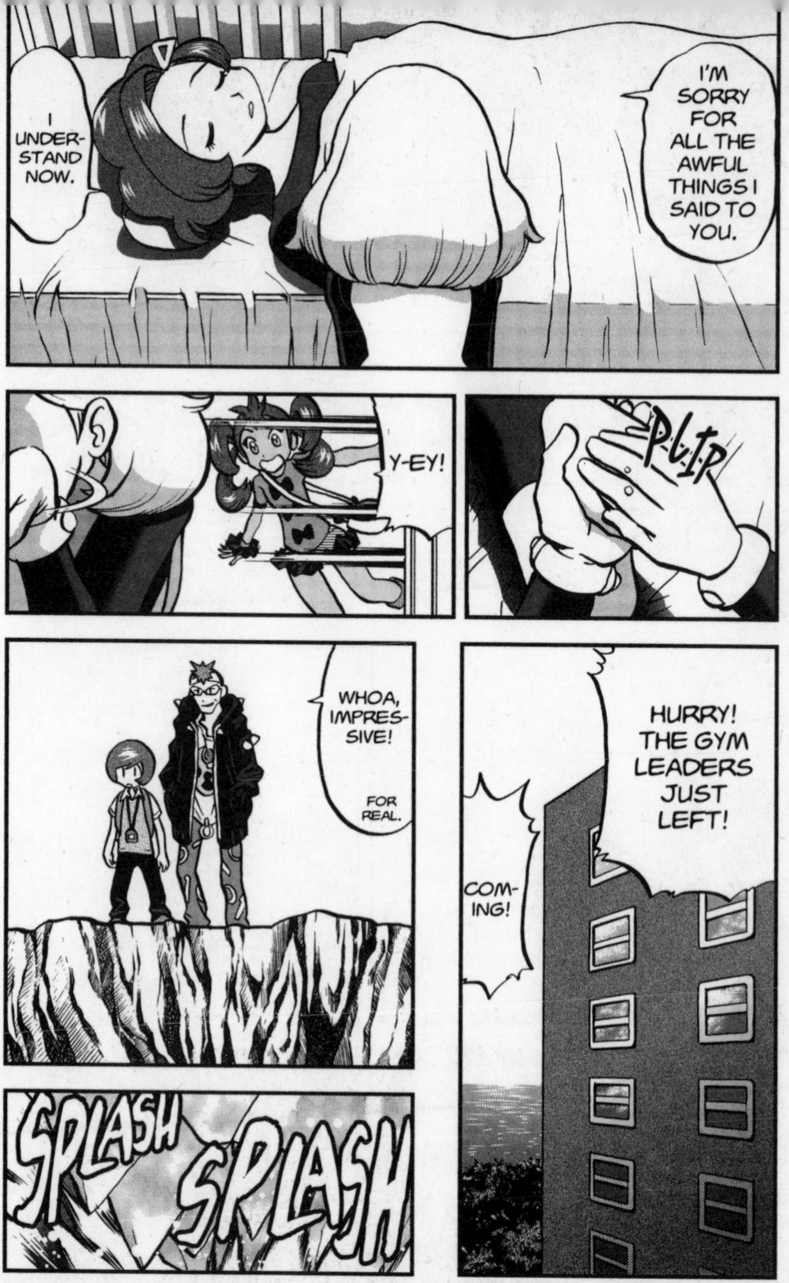
I'M SORRY FOR ALL THE AWFUL THINGS I SAID TO YOU.
I UNDER-STAND NOW.
P-L-I-P
Y-EY!
HURRY! THE GYM LEADERS JUST LEFT!
COM-ING!
WHOA, IMPRES-SIVE!
FOR REAL.
SPLASH
SPLASH

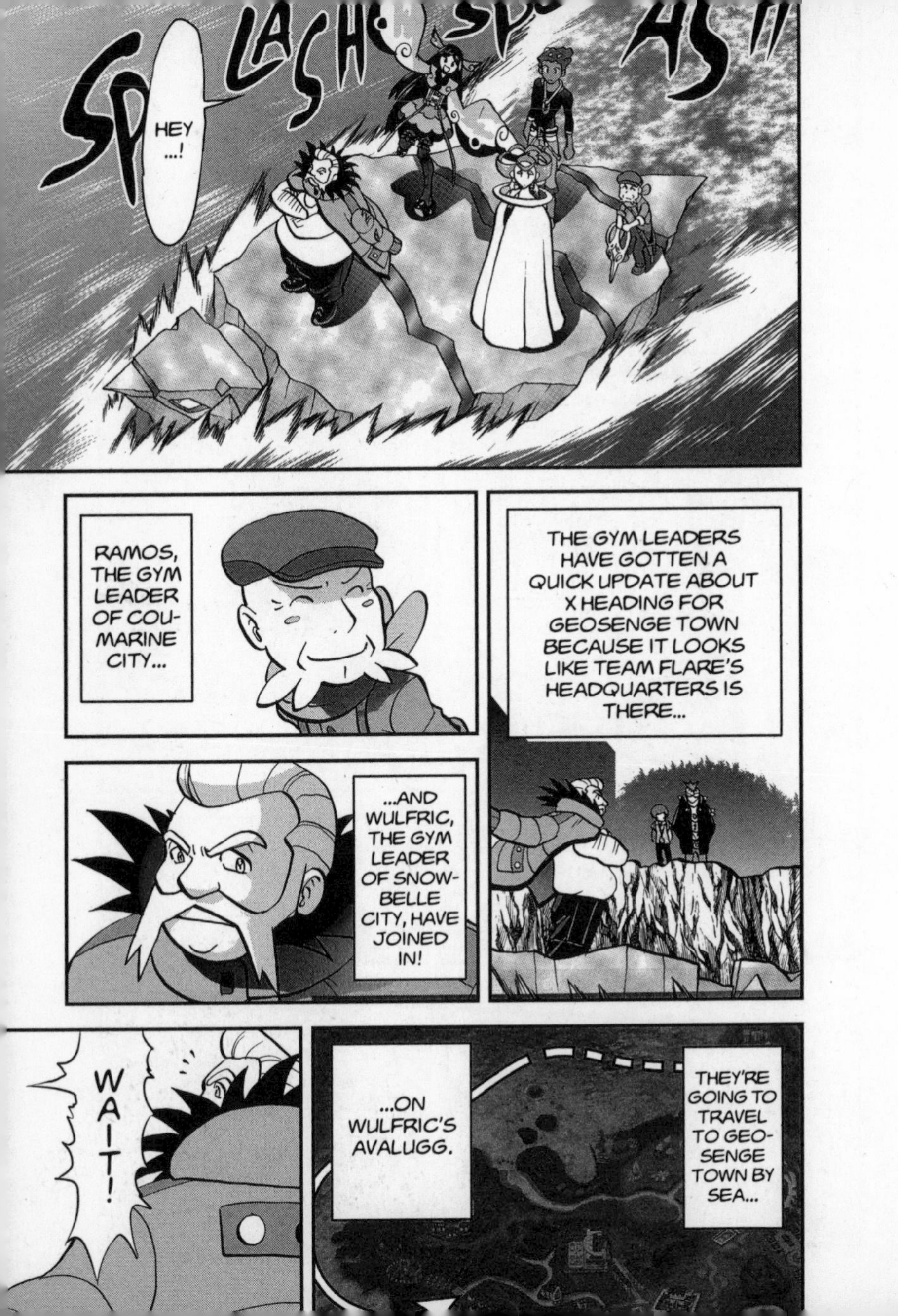
SPLASH SP AS!!
HEY ...!
THE GYM LEADERS HAVE GOTTEN A QUICK UPDATE ABOUT X HEADING FOR GEOSENGE TOWN BECAUSE IT LOOKS LIKE TEAM FLARE'S HEADQUARTERS IS THERE...
RAMOS, THE GYM LEADER OF COU-MARINE CITY...
...AND WULFRIC, THE GYM LEADER OF SNOW-BELLE CITY, HAVE JOINED IN!
THEY'RE GOING TO TRAVEL TO GEO-SENGE TOWN BY SEA...
...ON WULFRIC'S AVALUGG.
WAIT!

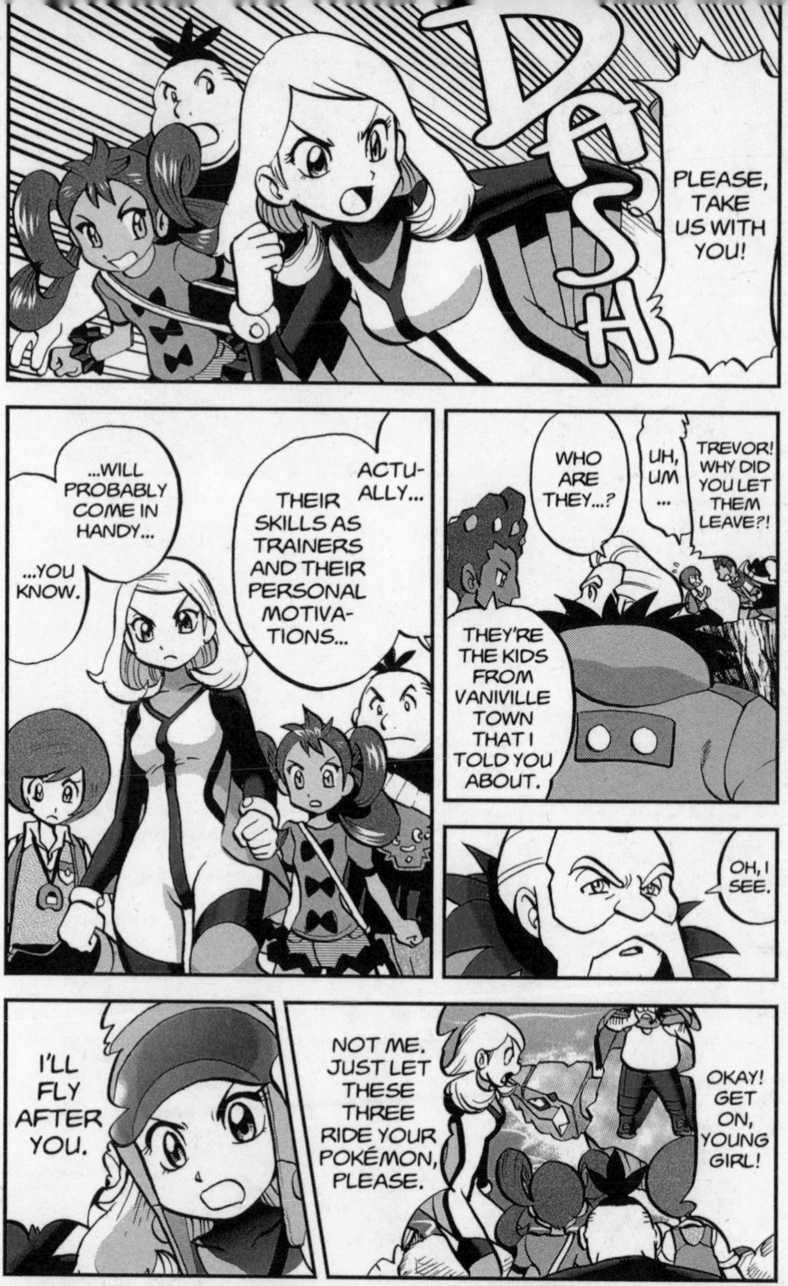
DASH
PLEASE, TAKE US WITH YOU!
TREVOR! WHY DID YOU LET THEM LEAVE?!
UH, UM ...
WHO ARE THEY...?
THEY'RE THE KIDS FROM VANIVILLE TOWN THAT I TOLD YOU ABOUT.
OH, I SEE.
ACTU-ALLY...
THEIR SKILLS AS TRAINERS AND THEIR PERSONAL MOTIVA-TIONS...
...WILL PROBABLY COME IN HANDY...
...YOU KNOW.
OKAY! GET ON, YOUNG GIRL!
NOT ME. JUST LET THESE THREE RIDE YOUR POKÉMON, PLEASE.
I'LL FLY AFTER YOU.

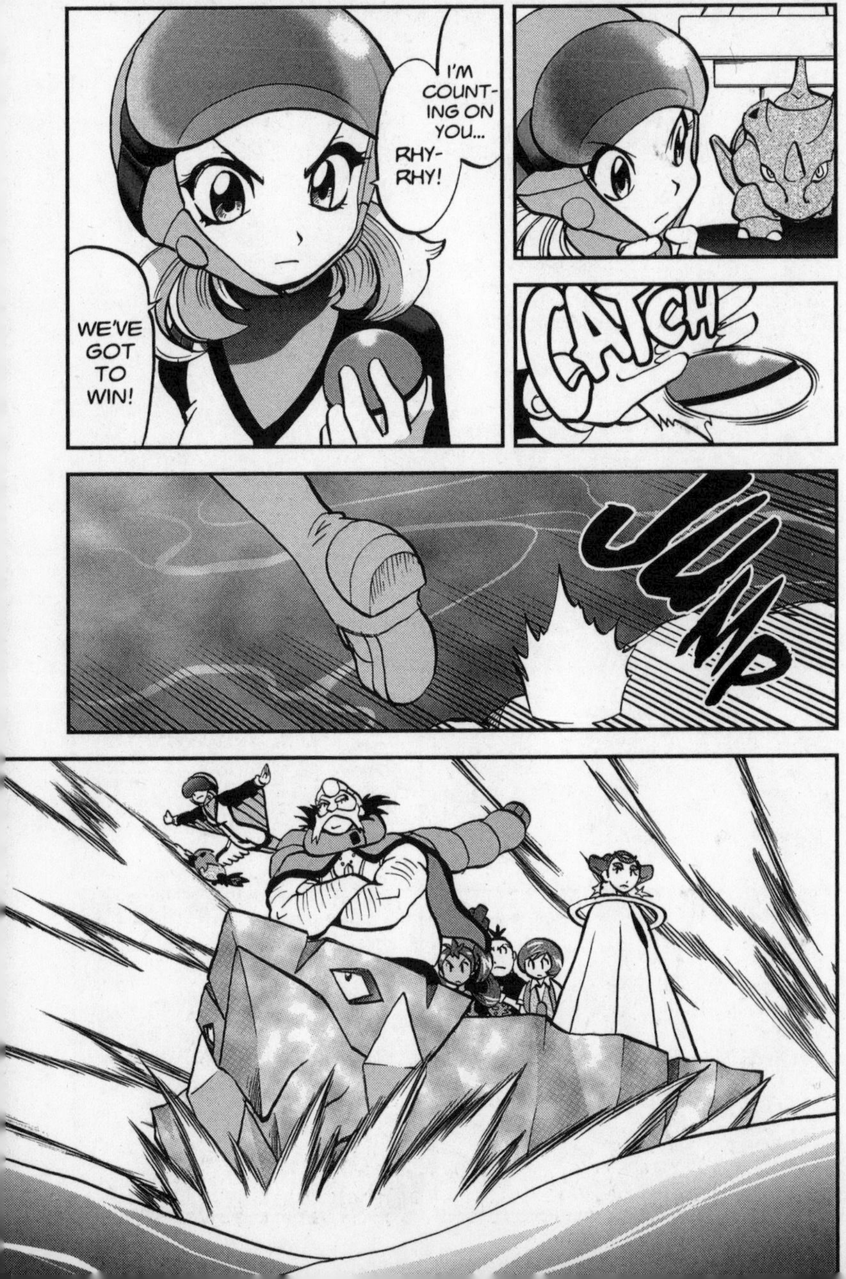
CATCH
I'M COUNTING ON YOU... RHY-RHY!
WE'VE GOT TO WIN!
JUMP

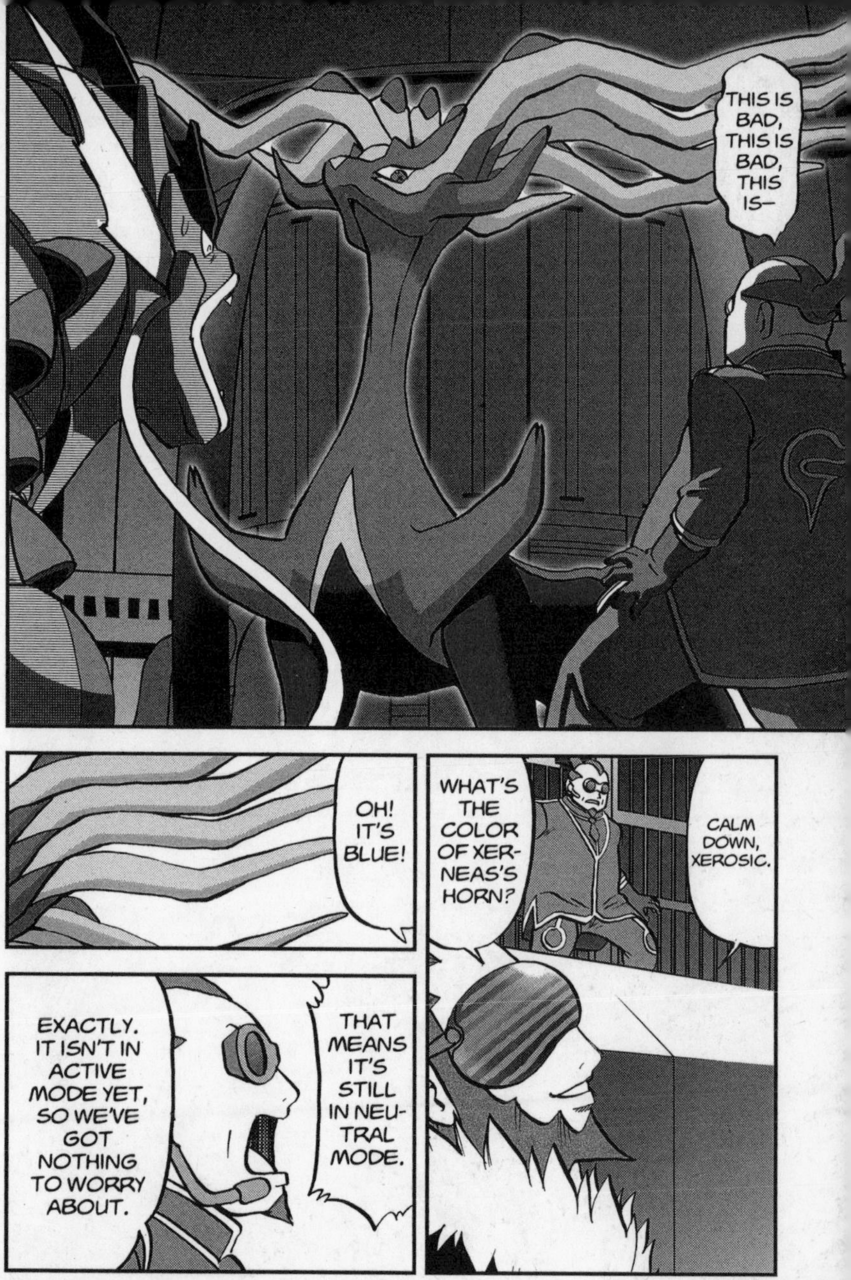
THIS IS BAD, THIS IS BAD, THIS IS—
CALM DOWN, XEROSIC.
WHAT'S THE COLOR OF XER-NEAS'S HORN?
OH! IT'S BLUE!
THAT MEANS IT'S STILL IN NEU-TRAL MODE.
EXACTLY. IT ISN'T IN ACTIVE MODE YET, SO WE'VE GOT NOTHING TO WORRY ABOUT.

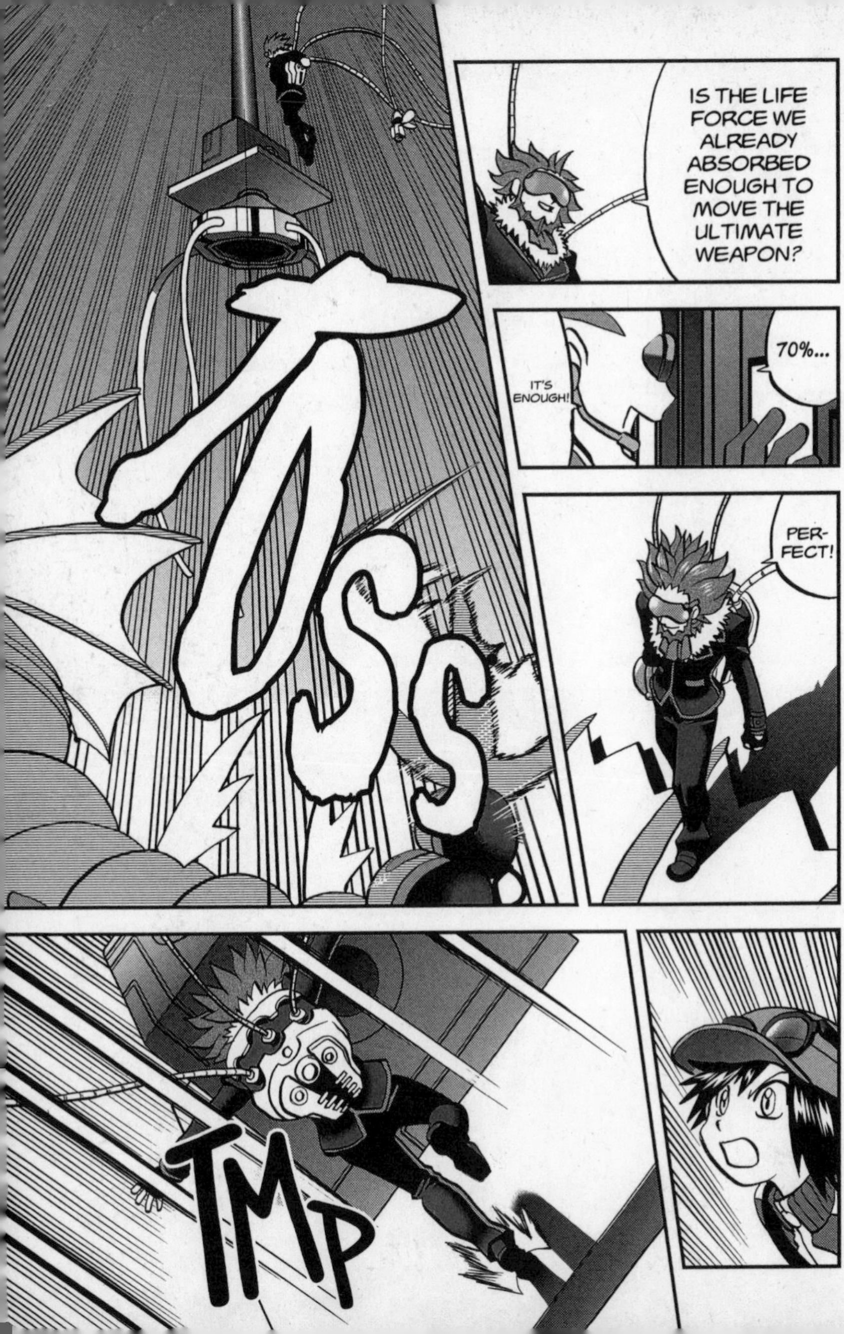
IS THE LIFE FORCE WE ALREADY ABSORBED ENOUGH TO MOVE THE ULTIMATE WEAPON?
70%...
IT'S ENOUGH!
PER-FECT!
TMP

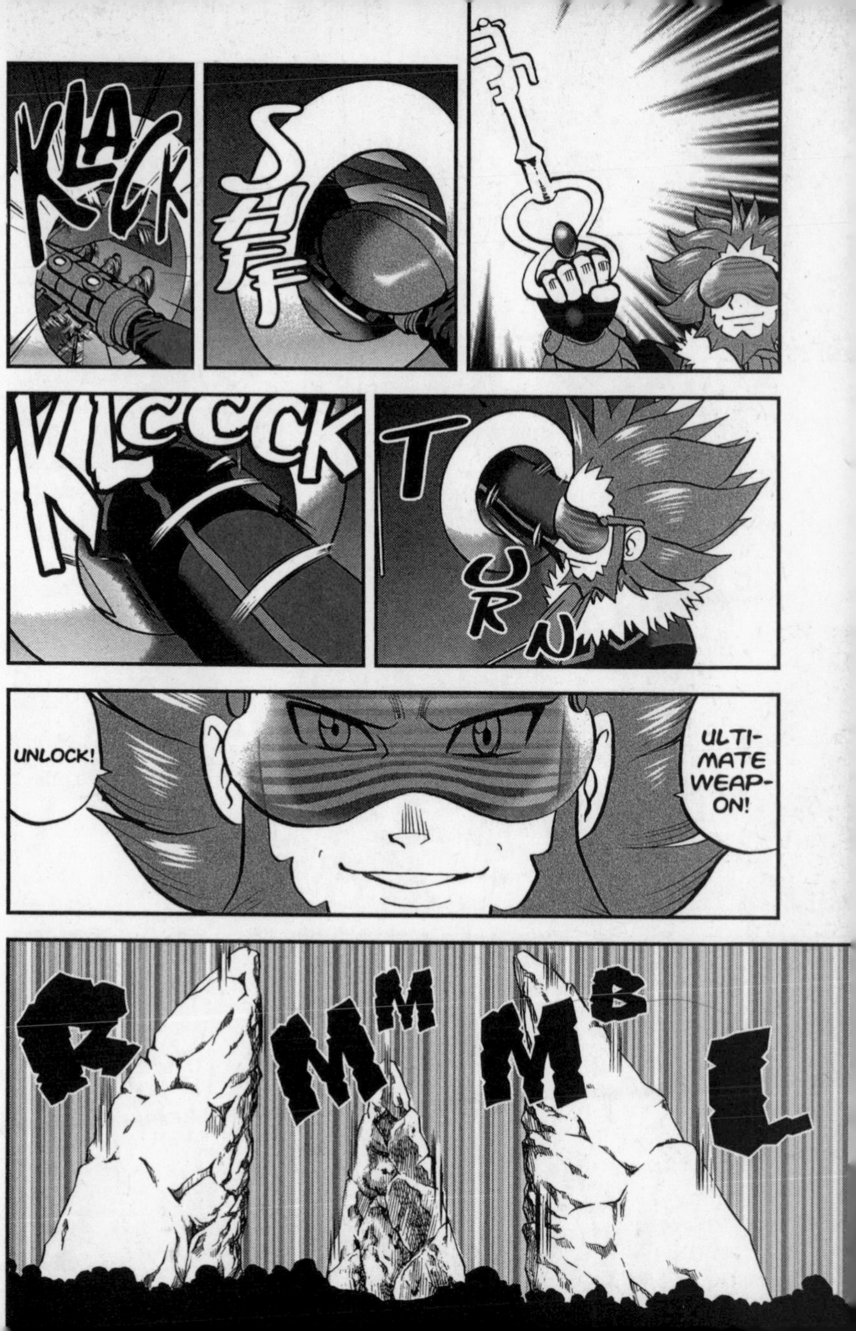
SHFFF
KLACK
TURN
KLCCCK
ULTI-
MATE
WEAP-
ON!
UNLOCK!
RMMMBL

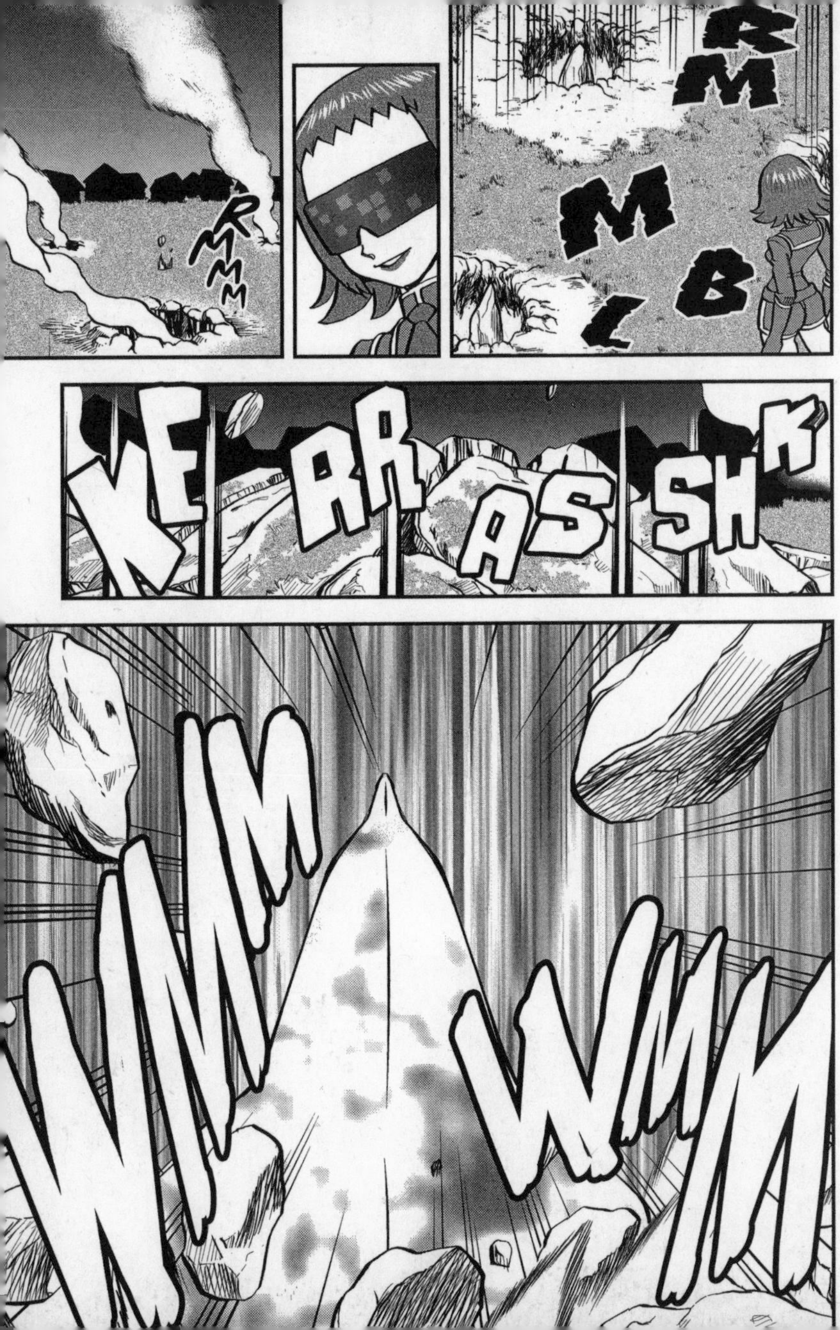
RMMMBL
RMMM
KERRASSHK
WMMM
WMMM

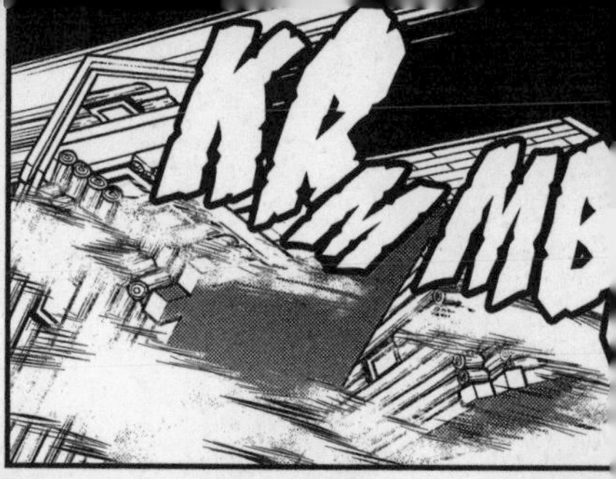
KRMMB
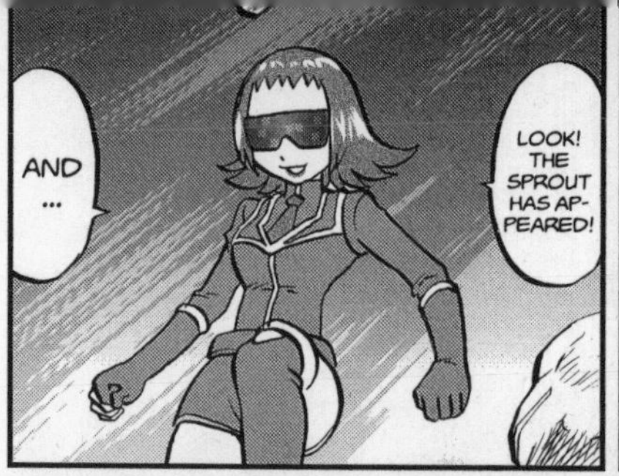
LOOK! THE SPROUT HAS AP-PEARED!
AND ...
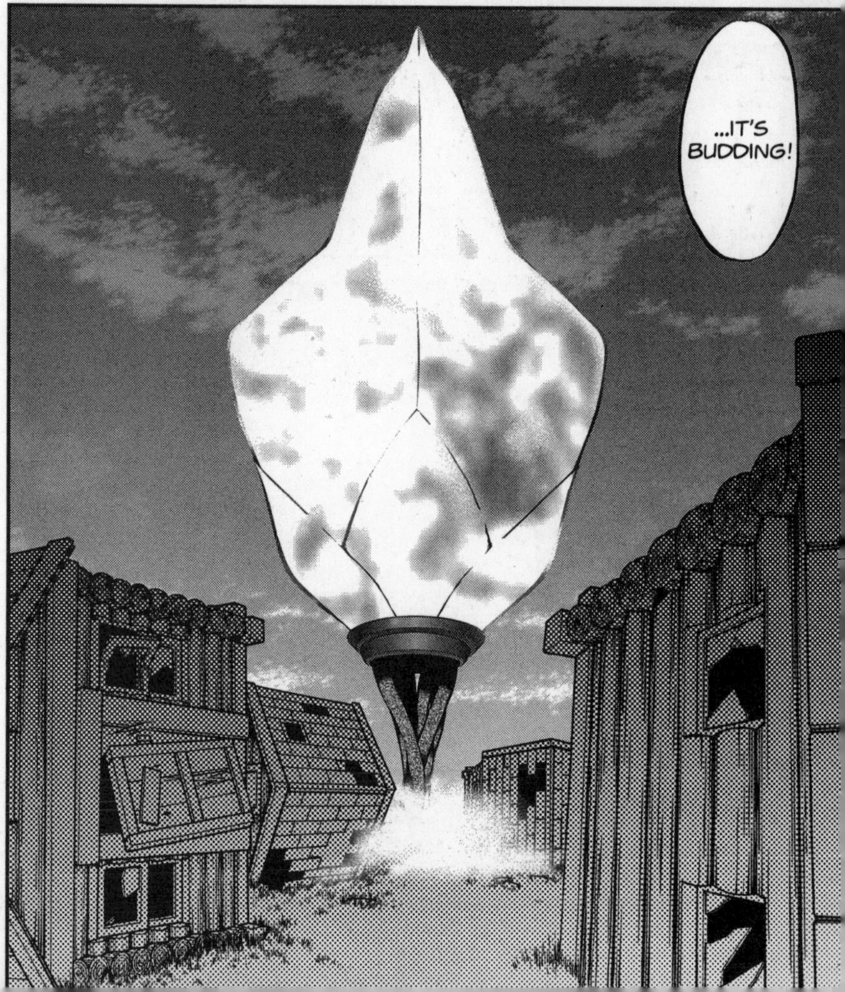
...IT'S BUDDING!

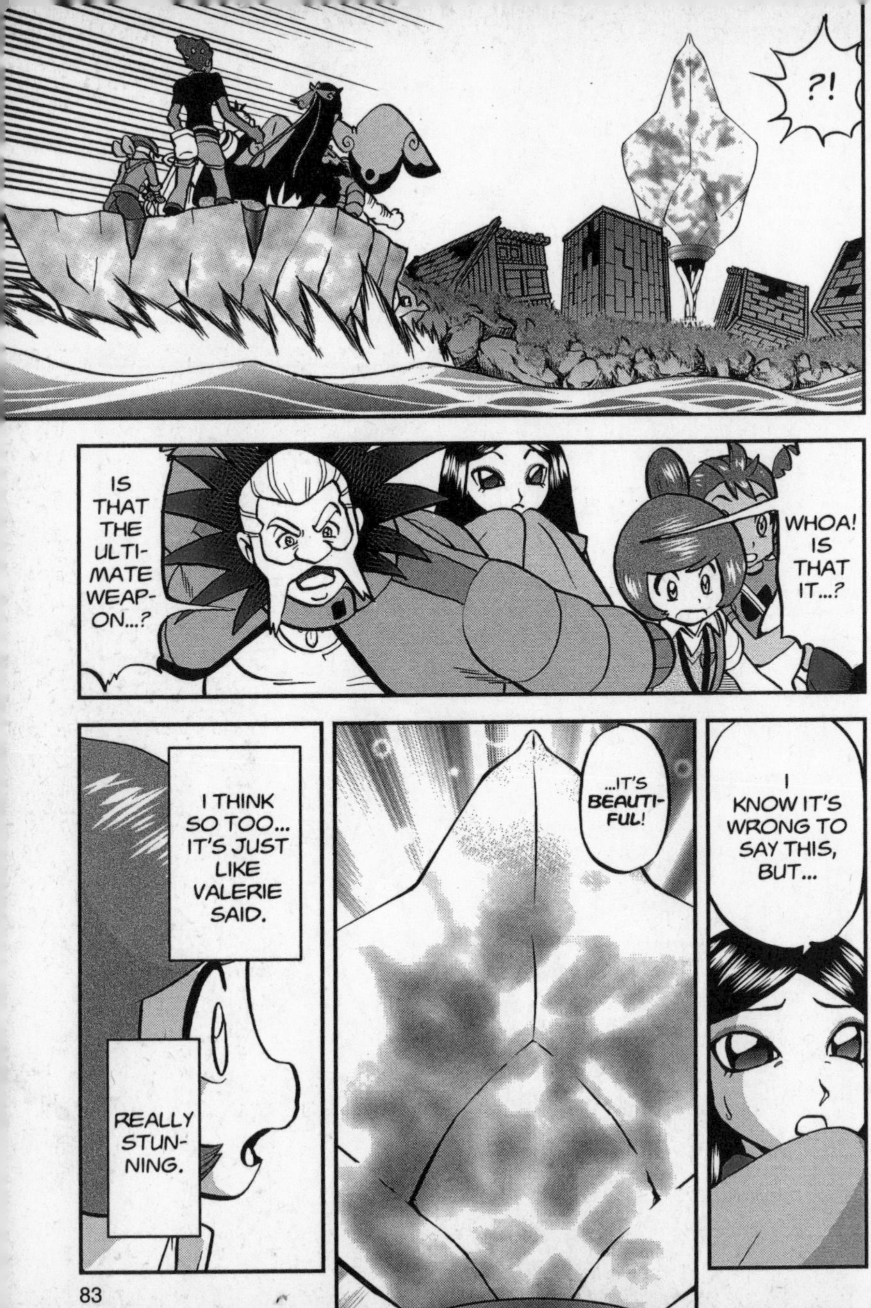
?!
WHOA! IS THAT IT...?
IS THAT THE ULTIMATE WEAPON...?
I KNOW IT'S WRONG TO SAY THIS, BUT...
...IT'S BEAUTIFUL!
I THINK SO TOO... IT'S JUST LIKE VALERIE SAID.
REALLY STUNNING.

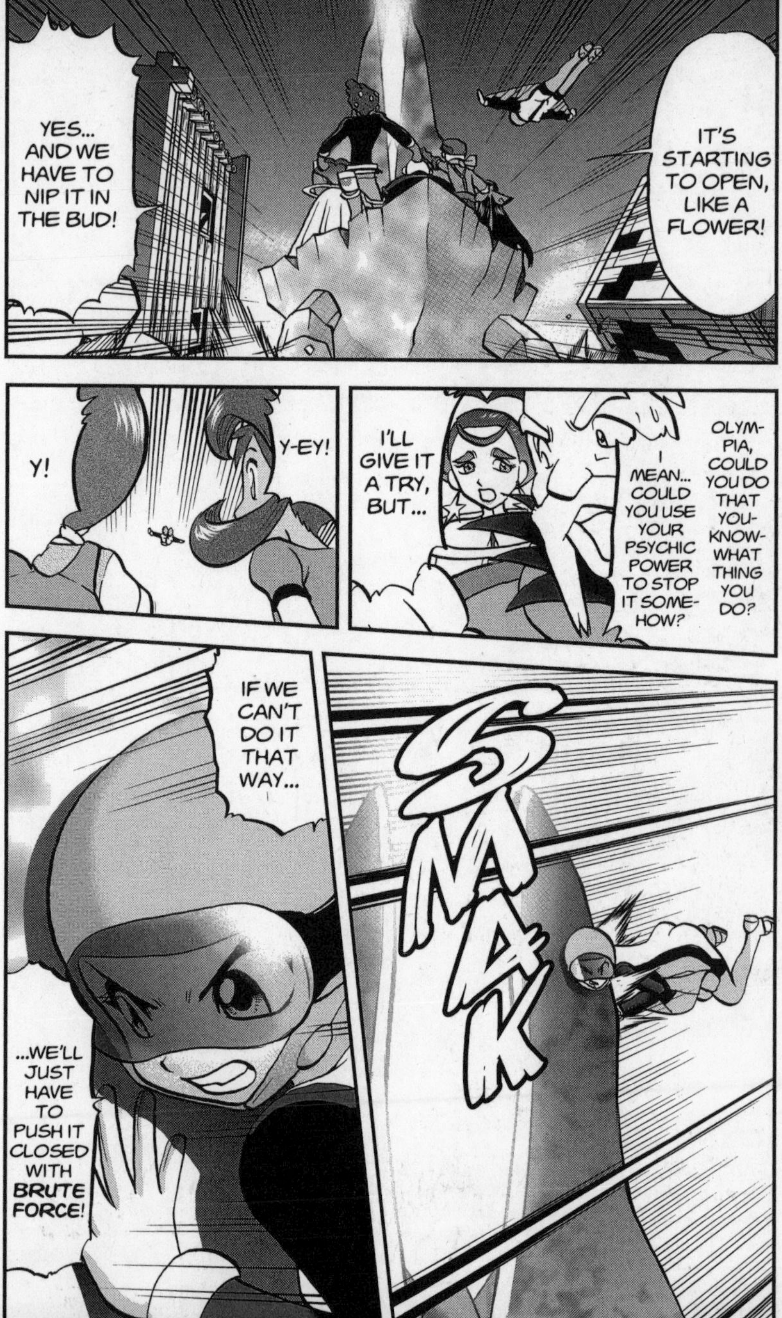
IT'S STARTING TO OPEN, LIKE A FLOWER!
YES... AND WE HAVE TO NIP IT IN THE BUD!
OLYM-PIA, COULD YOU DO THAT YOU-KNOW-WHAT THING YOU DO?
I MEAN... COULD YOU USE YOUR PSYCHIC POWER TO STOP IT SOME-HOW?
I'LL GIVE IT A TRY, BUT...
Y-EY!
Y!
SMAK
IF WE CAN'T DO IT THAT WAY...
...WE'LL JUST HAVE TO PUSH IT CLOSED WITH **BRUTE FORCE!**

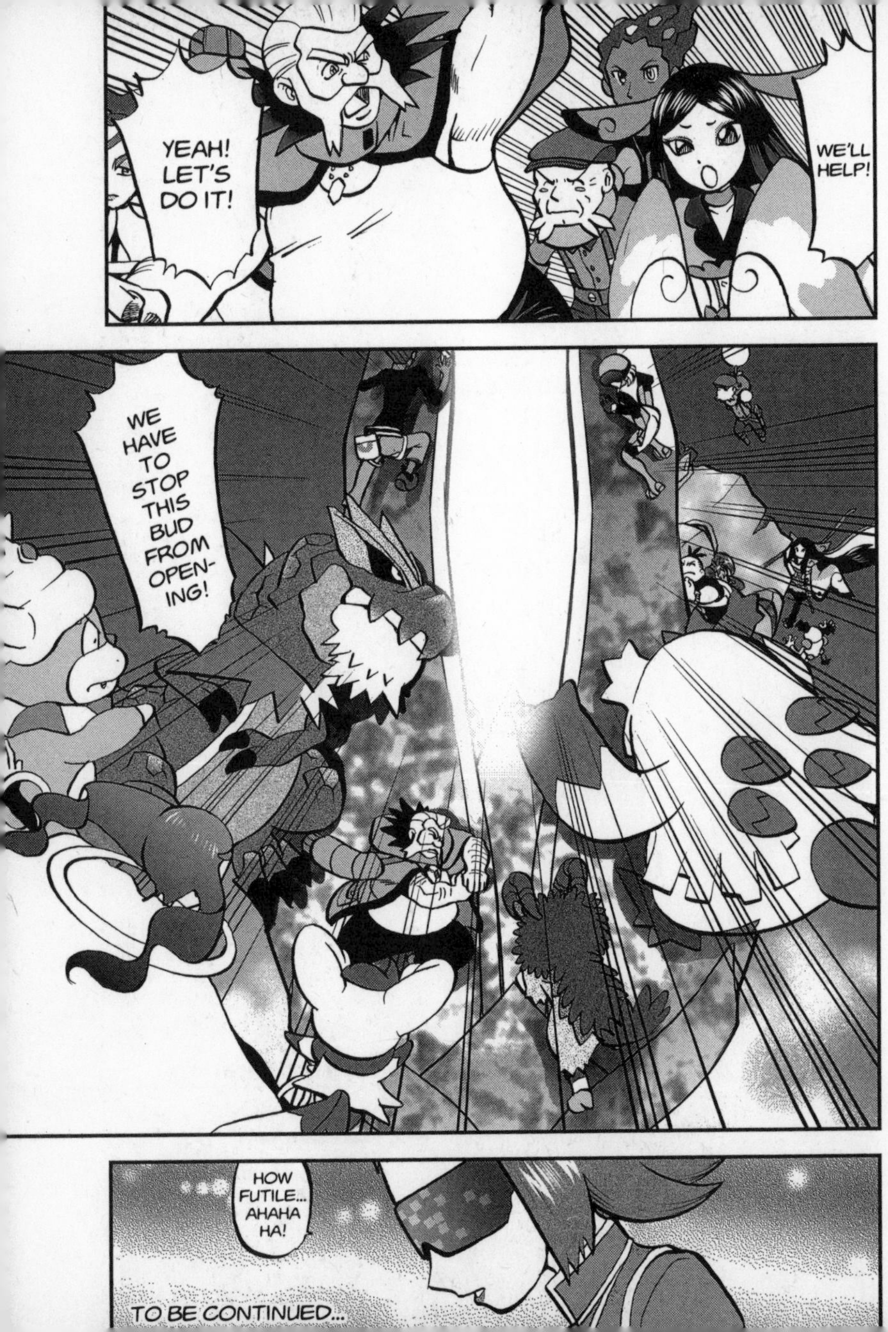
WE'LL HELP!
YEAH! LET'S DO IT!
WE HAVE TO STOP THIS BUD FROM OPEN-ING!
HOW FUTILE... AHAHA HA!
TO BE CONTINUED...

Current Location

Geosenge Town

A town lined with mysterious stones
and encircled by strange ruins of old.

Pokémon X • Y
Volume 7
Perfect Square Edition

Story by HIDENORI KUSAKA
Art by SATOSHI YAMAMOTO

©2016 Pokémon.
©1995-2016 Nintendo/Creatures Inc./GAME FREAK inc.
TM, ®, and character names are trademarks of Nintendo.
POCKET MONSTERS SPECIAL X•Y Vol. 4
by Hidenori KUSAKA, Satoshi YAMAMOTO
© 2014 Hidenori KUSAKA, Satoshi YAMAMOTO
All rights reserved.
Original Japanese edition published by SHOGAKUKAN.
English translation rights in the United States of America, Canada, the United
Kingdom, Ireland, Australia and New Zealand arranged with SHOGAKUKAN.

English Adaptation—Bryant Turnage
Translation—Tetsuichiro Miyaki
Touch-up & Lettering—Annaliese Christman
Design—Shawn Carrico
Editor—Annette Roman

Printed in the U.S.A.

Published by
VIZ Media, LLC
P.O. Box 77010
San Francisco, CA 94107

10 9 8 7 6 5 4 3 2 1
First printing, July 2016

PARENTAL ADVISORY
POKÉMON ADVENTURES
is rated A and is suitable
for readers of all ages.
ratings.viz.com

www.perfectsquare.com www.viz.com

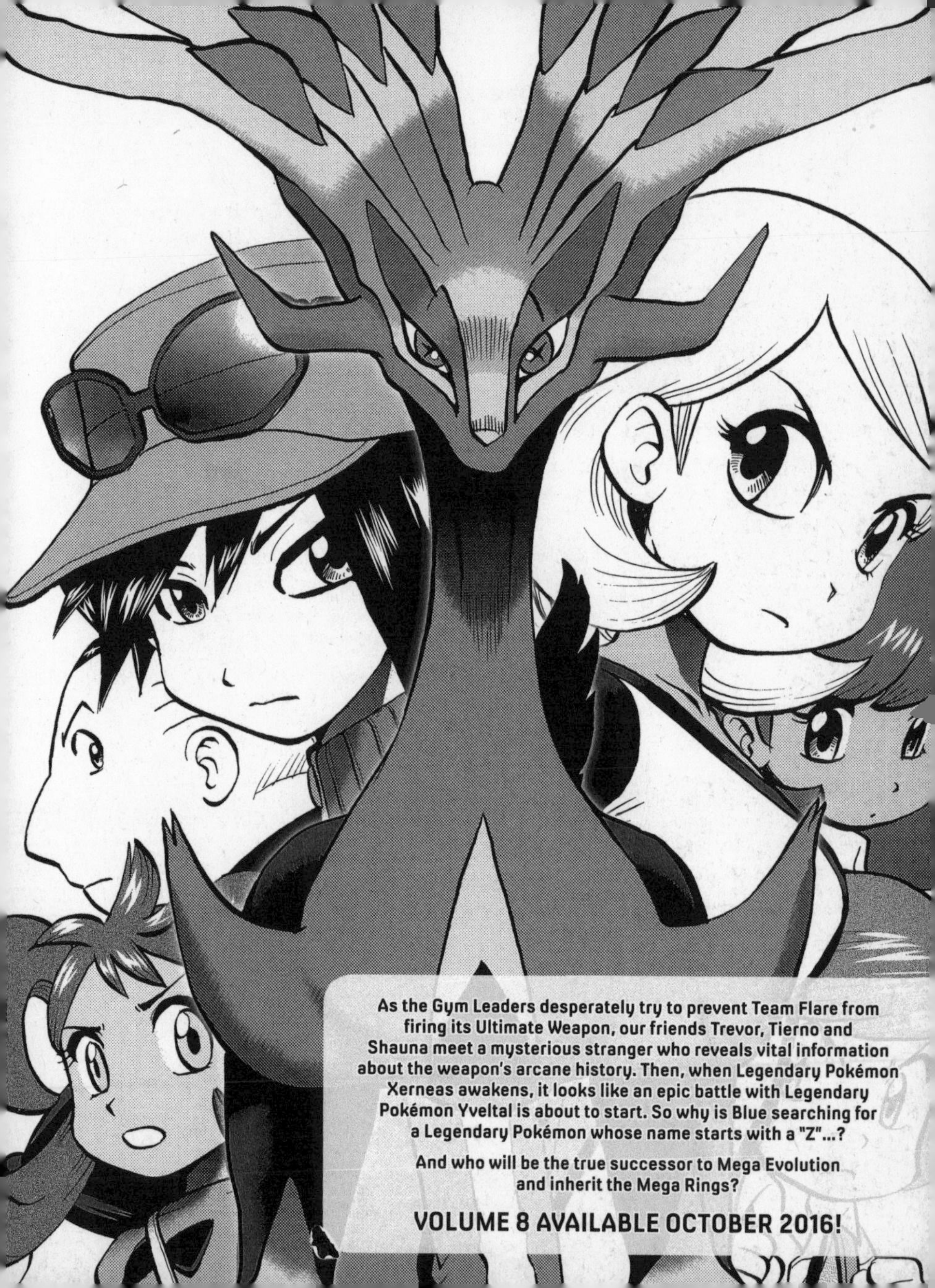
As the Gym Leaders desperately try to prevent Team Flare from firing its Ultimate Weapon, our friends Trevor, Tierno and Shauna meet a mysterious stranger who reveals vital information about the weapon's arcane history. Then, when Legendary Pokémon Xerneas awakens, it looks like an epic battle with Legendary Pokémon Yveltal is about to start. So why is Blue searching for a Legendary Pokémon whose name starts with a "Z"...?
And who will be the true successor to Mega Evolution and inherit the Mega Rings?
VOLUME 8 AVAILABLE OCTOBER 2016!

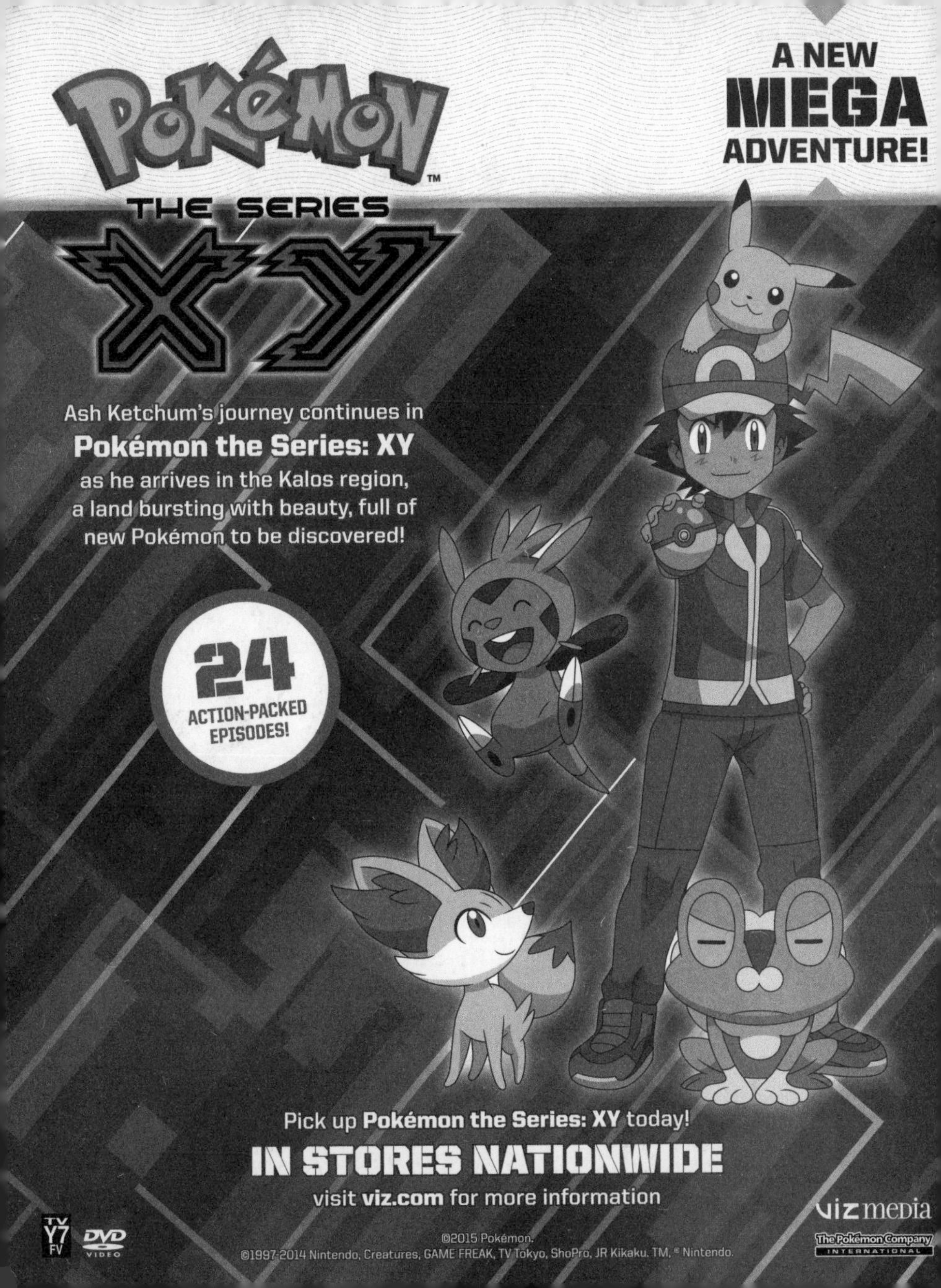

POKéMON™
THE SERIES
XY
A NEW
MEGA
ADVENTURE!
Ash Ketchum's journey continues in
Pokémon the Series: XY
as he arrives in the Kalos region,
a land bursting with beauty, full of
new Pokémon to be discovered!
24
ACTION-PACKED
EPISODES!
Pick up Pokémon the Series: XY today!
IN STORES NATIONWIDE
visit viz.com for more information
TV Y7 FV
DVD VIDEO
©2015 Pokémon.
©1997-2014 Nintendo, Creatures, GAME FREAK, TV Tokyo, ShoPro, JR Kikaku. TM, ® Nintendo.
viz media
The Pokémon Company INTERNATIONAL

BLACK & WHITE

STORY & ART BY **SANTA HARUKAZE**

YOUR FAVORITE POKÉMON FROM THE UNOVA REGION LIKE YOU'VE NEVER SEEN THEM BEFORE!

Available now!

A pocket-sized book brick jam-packed with four-panel comic strips featuring all the Pokémon Black and White characters, Pokémon vital statistics, trivia, puzzles, and fun quizzes!

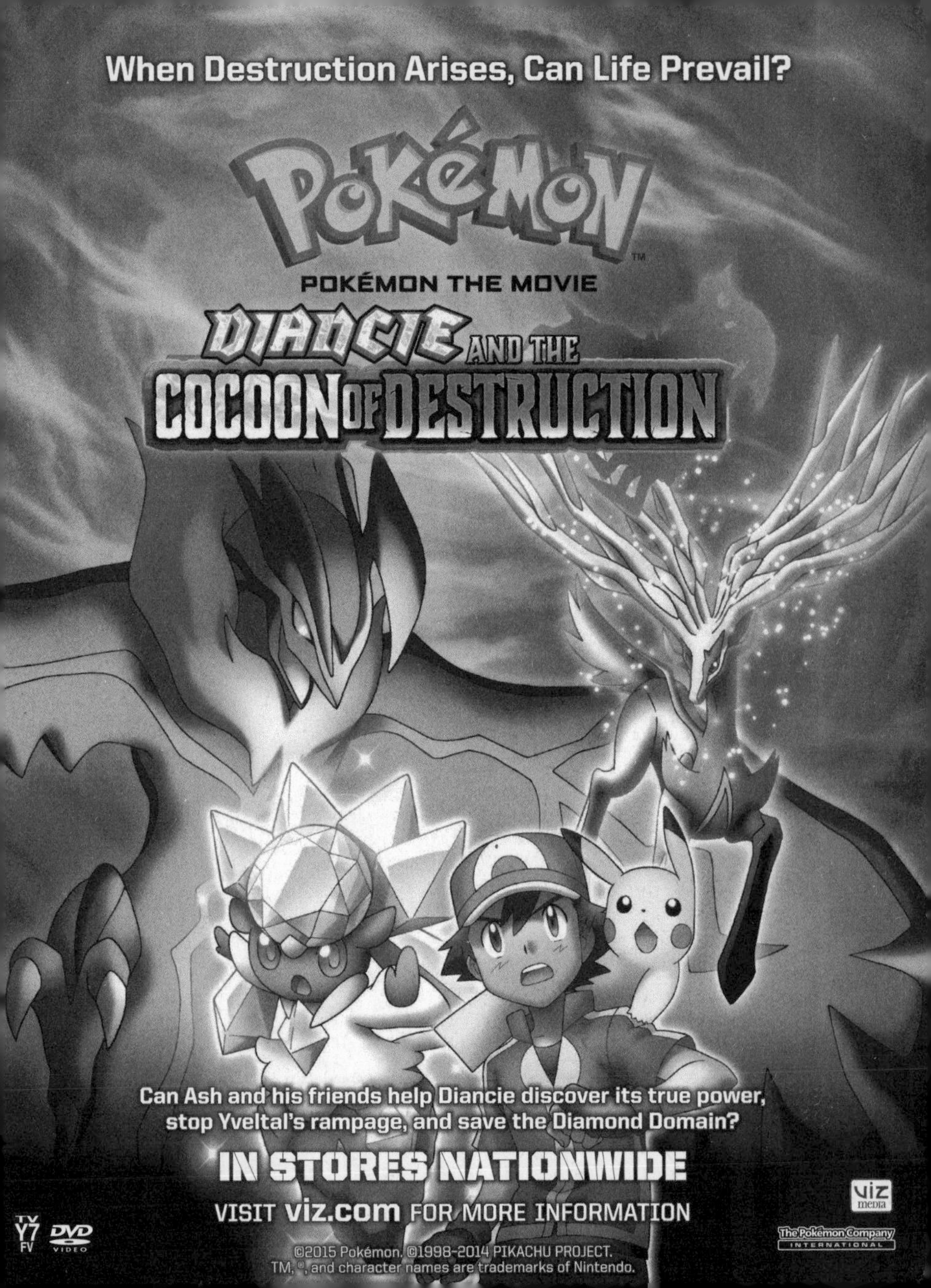
When Destruction Arises, Can Life Prevail?
POKÉMON™
POKÉMON THE MOVIE
DIANCIE AND THE COCOON OF DESTRUCTION
Can Ash and his friends help Diancie discover its true power, stop Yveltal's rampage, and save the Diamond Domain?
IN STORES NATIONWIDE
VISIT viz.com FOR MORE INFORMATION
TV Y7 FV
DVD VIDEO
VIZ media
The Pokémon Company INTERNATIONAL
©2015 Pokémon. ©1998-2014 PIKACHU PROJECT.
TM, ®, and character names are trademarks of Nintendo.

Begin your Pokémon Adventure here in the Kanto region!

POKÉMON™ ADVENTURES

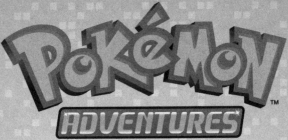

RED & BLUE BOX SET

Story by HIDENORI KUSAKA Art by MATO

POKÉMON
ADVENTURES
Bonus Poster Inside!
RED & BLUE BOX SET:
POKÉMON ADVENTURES VOLUMES 1-7

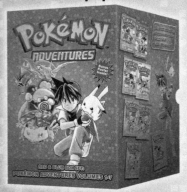

Includes POKÉMON ADVENTURES Vols. 1-7 and a collectible poster!

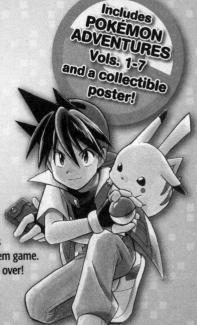

All your favorite Pokémon game characters jump out of the screen into the pages of this action-packed manga!

Red doesn't just want to train Pokémon, he wants to be their friend too. Bulbasaur and Poliwhirl seem game. But independent Pikachu won't be so easy to win over!

And watch out for Team Rocket, Red... They only want to be your enemy!

Start the adventure today!

VIZ media www.viz.com PERFECT SQUARE RATED A FOR ALL AGES ratings.viz.com

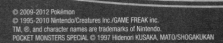

The adventure continues in the Johto region!

POKÉMON ADVENTURES
GOLD & SILVER BOX SET

Includes
POKÉMON ADVENTURES
Vols. 8-14
and a collectible poster!

Story by
HIDENORI KUSAKA

Art by
**MATO,
SATOSHI YAMAMOTO**

More exciting Pokémon adventures starring Gold and his rival Silver! First someone steals Gold's backpack full of Poké Balls (and Pokémon!). Then someone steals Prof. Elm's Totodile. Can Gold catch the thief—or thieves?!

Keep an eye on Team Rocket, Gold... Could they be behind this crime wave?

www.viz.com

THIS IS THE END OF THIS GRAPHIC NOVEL!

To properly enjoy this VIZ Media graphic novel, please turn it around and begin reading from right to left.

This book has been printed in the original Japanese format in order to preserve the orientation of the original artwork. Have fun with it!

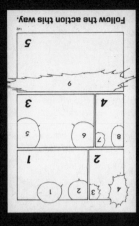

Follow the action this way.

‹‹‹ READ THIS WAY!